40 Single Gay

By

Jonathan Lee

40 Single Gay

Copyright © 2023 by Jonathan Lee.

The events and conversations in this book have been set down to the best of the author's ability, although some names and details have been changed to protect the privacy of individuals.

Second Edition: May 2023

10 9 8 7 6 5 4 3 2

Chapter 1

Birthday Celebrations

On my 40th birthday I wake up in my childhood bedroom, which still hosts zebra print squares and the Friends TV series wallpaper strip interlaced with newspaper glossed to the wall. My bed is squeaky – not from any action I got from my teenage years, as I was a bit of a late bloomer to say the least – but simply from age, something I'm also starting to feel now. I would be alone if it were not for my dog, Raff who stirs once he sees I'm awake, and the prospect of kibbles becomes apparent.

There is a knock at the door and before there's

time to say 'come in,' or 'go away,' which would be my preferred response, my mum enters with a cup of tea.

'Happy birthday love … the big four zero, how do you feel?' This is a question you get used to, as if somehow your life changes at midnight and you have a whole new perspective, a whole new mindset and new way of being. In reality, you feel no different. I felt like shit when I went to bed at 8.30pm last night as I couldn't face another evening watching the soaps with my mother, and that is how I feel now. I didn't sleep at 8.30 though, instead I saw every hour of the night go by.

Let me introduce myself, my name is Jonathan Lee. I'm forty years old, six days single after being dumped by my ex whilst we were having sex – I know! There is a certain vulnerability you feel when you are told you are only seventy percent of what the other person is looking for whilst naked, and I reckon I'm in an exclusive group of people to experience this. Despite this accolade I'm still a pretty unremarkable person, all things considered. If I'm being honest, I think we could say that about most people in life, at least I'm not deluding myself. I was deluding myself thinking I had met the one. One fuckwit more like. I have varying feelings when I think of him; mostly anger, some betrayal, sadness, a lot of sadness, love and emptiness. Mostly I just feel nothing. I'm not going to go on about him now, that's not going to be fun to read. I will address this at one point, but I'm not quite ready to do this yet.

Right, this is where I start to sound a bit creepy. Remember I was only dumped one week ago, and that pain can make you do some crazy things. Well, it made me. I created a Grindr profile. Not to start my new life of being a singleton again, or as an eligible bachelor as my mum puts it, but in order to stalk my ex. That person who once loved me, or so he said. I was intrigued to see if he was online and dating already, and yes smack bang in front of me was his profile, looking all chiselled face, handsome and smug. I added his profile to favourites so at the touch of a button I could see when he was online, where in the country he was, what he was looking for – this was always no strings sex, and so I could just plumet to a new depth of darkness feeling more miserable and alone.

I know it is the absolute worst thing I can do but I just can't stop myself, I'm not ready to let go and move on, instead I watch his whereabouts relentlessly. Each square he moves from. When he's online I imagine him having this explicit text sex exchange of filth and smut, and when he is not online I think he is actually having sex and imagine him riding some dark stallion with a big broad hairy chest and hung dick. Maybe he has a big handlebar moustache too? Anyway, he is more of a man than me. Perhaps he's called Hank, or something like that. So how do I feel?

'I feel so much better for that sleep. Sorry for going to bed so early, I just felt so tired from all that driving,' I politely explain to my mum.

'Of course not love, that's everything catching up with you. Glad you slept well though, didn't I say things would be better in the morning.'

So that's what I said, but what I really thought was – I feel like absolute crap, like a little module of poop stuck to the leg of a dung beetle. This image is now racing through my mind, is it doing the same in yours?

I didn't expect to be single at forty. That was not part of the plan. Getting to this point in my life, successful career, nice home and good health, although last week I started smoking again after quitting fifteen years ago but I'm still fit. I felt completely side bombed by the revelation that I was only seventy percent of what he was looking for. Seventy, that's like a B in most GCSE exams, isn't it? Or whatever number it is now. Scoring a B is good. Clearly not good enough, and that's how I feel on my 40th birthday as I continue to lie on this squeaky bed with my Shih-Tzu Cross Pug Whippet dog – I know you can't make it up – now licking my face and blowing dog breath in my eyes.

Back to my amazing birthday. Having established that I wake up alone, I should really be waking up with Adam and his big muscly arms and six pack where we then have wild morning sex showing little regard for bed head or morning breath. Fresh coffee and an assortment of presents should await being opened, all displayed on the white Egyptian cotton bedsheets; some small gifts, some big, a few little humorous ones alongside a lovingly thoughtful main present which sums up Adam's complete love and devotion for me. I still have the bed head and bad breath from the fags I was smoking from the window; a throwback to my youth and a reminder that despite the years, I have not moved on at all, being in the exact same position I was twenty-two years ago. I bet he's having sex now.

I leave my bedroom and stumble to the kitchen to find my mum watching breakfast television. She comments that she loves the presenter's hair whilst she delivers news of a local disaster where a Spanish family were knocked down by a bus and they all died.

'It is nice,' I reply, 'you could have hair like that.' I see my mum reflect and ponder and after a good two minutes she agrees. I feed Raff, promptly finish my cup of tea and then explain that he needs walking so I'm going to do that first.

'What about your card and presents?'

'I'll open them later, when I'm back.'

'Okay my love, see you in a bit.'

As soon as I'm out of eyesight I reach for my

phone. There is a green dot next to Adam's name so I know he's online, the fucker. He would rather chat to Hank or Marco or Stavros than wish me a happy birthday. My stomach is in knots with anger. A feeling I'm not all that familiar with. Generally, I'm a laid back person. I get that from my dad, and his work ethic, I get that from him too, but I was blindsided to the split which has made me feel a fool and now left me questioning everything. Raff stops for a pee and a sniff, he does this a lot. At least I have Raff in my life, the little fluff bag. He was my dog, I got him a year before meeting Adam. I do question whether Adam loved Raff more than me at times. I also question whether Raff loves Adam more than me. I question that a lot. They had a bond, they would play. Raff loved giving spot bruises to Adam. He would follow him around, I guess he does that to me too. He would wait at the balcony doors and would recognise the sound of Adam's car. I assume he does that for me. Anyhow, the point is he's a bundle of fluff who despite the dog breath gives the best cuddles.

We go to the beach where I used to walk my childhood dog, Bow. Oh I miss her, a gorgeous golden retriever. I sometimes wish Bow and Raff could meet, merging the two parts of my life, then and now. They would get on, I'm sure. It's strange walking along the same sand where I once would have stepped as a child. Yeah, I'm definitely in a reflective mood. Partly due to turning forty and partly because of the recent dumping episode. I grew up in a small seaside town in Cornwall. Yes, I miss it and plan to return to live there one day. A commonly asked question. Growing up in Cornwall was lovely, idyllic you could say, but as someone coming to terms with their sexuality it did feel a bit claustrophobic so at eighteen I escaped the small town for a bigger city. Not that I took advantage of this freedom. I was never that adventurous and tended to favour the quieter, more sedate things in life. Boring some might say.

The walk has not changed, a few parts are overgrown in places but in the twenty odd years I have been visiting this provides a sense of stability. I can't get Adam out of my mind, thinking how he seamlessly is able to move on with his life. It was not completely perfect with him, even I knew it was not one hundred percent. It was a complicated relationship to say the least and we had previously broken up on several occasions which is why when we last got back together, four months ago, we agreed that we couldn't keep yoyoing like this and would be honest and open with how we were feeling. This did not happen, well not until last week when Adam delivered the fatal stab. Whereas before, the splits seemed more mutual. We both reached a point of common understanding and acceptance. Then despite this we couldn't stay apart and would find excuses to see each other again and rekindle the love we had. Have. No had. I don't know. This time it feels different, this feels more final which leaves me unexpectedly alone at forty.

I go to check my phone again and just as I do I hear a ping. It's a text message from Adam.

'Happy Birthday, sorry it's not the best start to your 40th but hope you still have an amazing day with your family.' Is he for real? Not the best start. That's an understatement and a half, no that's an understatement and seventy percent. And does he not know me at all? I'm spending it with my family so he knows it's not going to be an amazing day. In fact, I sometimes question how well he did know me. He would often make me tea with loads of milk. How could he not remember that I have a splash, not even a splash, a teaspoon, hardly worth putting it in as I would often explain in coffee shops. He couldn't remember this? Then I would have English Breakfast tea up until midday, then change to Earl Grey. The number of mornings I would wake to Earl Grey. I'm sounding ungrateful here, it's lovely someone making you a drink, but you would think they would remember your preferences. Having said that I could most definitely drink a milky Earl Grey tea now.

I ponder for all of five seconds. The sensible me would not reply and reflect for a bit longer. However, I cannot manage this. In fact, the night before I anticipated this would happen so had previously written a reply and saved it in the notes app on my phone. I may be socially awkward (his words, kind of, I'm paraphrasing a bit) and inept (again my perception, what he actually said may have been slightly different), I may only be seventy percent (he definitely said this), but you cannot question my organisational skills. Fail to prepare, prepare to fail is my motto. Oh shut up, why am I sharing that? Anyway, back to my reply.

'I don't hear from you in a week and then you casually send me a text message wishing me a happy fucking birthday. I won't be having an amazing birthday as I feel completely side balled by you breaking up with me. I know we said we would keep some distance between us but I thought you would have at least asked how I'm doing earlier.' Send. Heart flutters. Return feelings of anger, and sadness. Oh yes, there's that feeling of sadness too.

I light another cigarette, this will be my third so far. Phone pings. 'I'm sorry you feel that, I do still love you and have found this all very hard blah blah blah.' I can't be bothered to reply, my energy levels feel low and I'm still trying to work out what is going on. I haven't cried, that's different from last time, I think the anger I'm feeling is preventing me from doing this. My rational self knows that the relationship was flawed, that Adam may not had been completely right for me, that perhaps we were not the best match, but my emotions are one of loss. Loss of friendship, more than that, loss of a lover. Don't get me wrong, I'm a strong person, I'm fine in my own company but right now, I just want to be held.

Chapter 2

Birthday celebrations continue

Back at my mum's house and my dad, sister and nieces arrive. My nieces make posters and balloons and have arranged a table of cards and presents. It's very sweet but I cannot allow myself to enjoy this day. Ordinarily I would just binge watch a series on Netflix, not talk to anyone and just cuddle Raff. It's my 40th so I'm forced to be sociable. Don't get me wrong, my family are lovely, I love them deeply, but we have never been a close family, so it doesn't feel natural to share my feelings, but the magnitude of this misery is also too much to mask.

Let's dissect the 'lovely vs not close family' statement – I guess I've always felt different to my family. Like they don't really get me. Perhaps my sister gets me most but even that's at a distance. And that's how I feel, at a distance to them. They are a family who would rarely say 'I love you.' The only time my mum would say it is when I'm about to step inside a plane and she fears I'll be involved in a crash. I don't think I've ever heard my dad or sister mutter the phrase. It'd be alien to start sharing my feelings now, despite being constantly asked, 'how am I feeling?' and that 'it is ok to talk about it?'

'Uncle Jonathan, open your cards first.'

'Okay,' I say.

Being around young children is difficult for me. I'm just going to come out and say it. I don't like children. They are too unpredictable. I like my own space and children are not respectful of that. They climb over me at times, jump on my lap, follow me around. This is acceptable when Raff does it, but not children. Although that is an advantage I've found to having a dog, my nieces will prod, play with, and cuddle him now. Most of the time anyway.

I open my first card, it is a personalised one from my sister and reads, 'Happy Birthday Jonathan, 40 years loved Then and Now'. There's an image of me as a two-year-old child and a recent photograph of me and Raff. Instantly I feel choked. I don't know what it is, but seeing those two images side by side, the young innocent boy with his whole future ahead of him, and the forty-year-old struggling to understand who he is and where he is in the world. I start to cry, and when I say cry, I mean floods. Sobbing like a baby, tears usually only seen when watching Long Lost Families.

'Why is Uncle Jonathan crying?' I hear. I have to leave the room in fear of being comforted, I tell myself to pull it together, not to be so stupid and then I decide to just be, and allow the tears to pour down my face as I think of that two-year-old child with his whole future ahead of him, and just what I have become.

Once composed I continue to open presents. Normally it's something I would get excited about and allow my inner child to take centre stage. At what point should a person feel like a grown up? I'm now forty but don't feel it. I wonder if that's the case for most people. Okay, present time from my sister. It's a gift experience day for two. Hmmm, it does feel like salt being rubbed into the wound. Shall I take my dreamy boyfriend with me? Clearly, she didn't know we were going to break up. Hell, I didn't know we were going to split. She was disappointed too, my family loved

Adam. The next gift opened is hotel spa voucher, again, for two. I smile recognising the irony. I leave the remainder of the presents to open another time. There's only so much excitement one can take.

Despite the efforts made by my family I can't enjoy my birthday. I find it difficult to make conversation and pretend to be interested in what is going on around me. This is difficult as being the birthday boy, the focus is all about me. I do, however, make it through the day. A family BBQ in mum's garden. Whenever there is food around, so there is Raff, so this works to my advantage where the attention goes on him for a bit. I'm there but not present, and all I can think about is returning home to where I can close the door to my flat and escape the fires of this world.

Midway through the day I do reply to Adam. There is a softening in the text messages where we acknowledge the holes in the relationship and the love we still hold for each other. We agree that we need our own space to heal and make sense of how we are feeling. Previously when we had parted, we vowed to remain close friends. In fact, I describe this as my superpower, my ability to remain friends with my exes. Not that I've had loads, just two significant others. Now three. This was different. I think it is because I still have feelings for him. Whereas with Tom and Steve, my previous partners, I was pleased when they met other people and moved on with their lives, the thought of Adam with someone makes me feel sick. I know this as I imagine him constantly in different sexual scenarios with different men. This reminds me, I'd better check my phone again. Why am I doing this to myself? It's punishment. Is it because I feel responsible for the breakup because I was not enough, so I need to experience this pain again and again, or is it that I just want to be close to him again? Even if it is as a bystander watching the new life that he is creating. The new exciting and promiscuous life, at least in my imagination anyway. I look at my phone. The green dot is there, he is still explaining to Hank in graphic detail that he wants to ride him. 'You're going to start slow, and then I want you to push it in deep, deep and hard as I ride you bare.'

There is one last birthday celebration, I use the term 'celebration' loosely, before I get to leave. My family have booked a meal at the local Meadery. Now for anyone who has not heard of a Meadery, they are medieval themed restaurants in Cornwall apparently famous for their atmosphere which consists of being lit by candlelight alone, you don't eat with cutlery just your hands (they do however give you a little bowl of water with a slice of lemon to clean your hands), food served on wooden plates, quite basic food I guess of ribs, 'chicken in the rough' (fried chicken) and fish fries. Oh, and you are served by women dressed as wenches. Well, that's nice that Adam's mum was able to join me for my birthday celebrations after all. Bitch never liked me.

It's a place of my childhood and one that I still hold as a guilty pleasure. If you have not been to a Meadery before than I urge you to try it. This, however, is not quite the glamorous white party that I had started to plan for my 40th as I sit next to my incredibly racist uncle one side of me and one of my nieces on the other. She insisted on sitting next to Uncle Jonathan only to scream and cry over the darkness of the restaurant and not wanting to have anything on the menu. The mead wine saves me as I slowly get drunk as a mechanism to make it through the night, which I just about do.

The next morning, it is time for just one cup of tea before I set off. I still feel rubbish. The past few days has been so awkward which is a metaphor for how I feel. Adam used to call it quirkiness but that was really just a polite way of saying weird. Why was he with me for two years if I was such a weirdo? Did he just feel sorry for me? And then what changed? I feel used. During the first eighteen months of our relationship Adam lived with his ex and described the arrangement as a toxic atmosphere which they were stuck with as they tried to sell their house. I wasn't weird then, then I wasn't too quiet. It was not until he moved

JONATHAN LEE

and started to feel more confident in his own place did he voice his concerns about the relationship. Of course it was more complicated than this, so many more layers which I don't think either of us will understand, but it's only been a week and I'm still pissed about it.

My time down in Cornwall was laden with memories; the towns and villages we visited as a couple, the walks we went on, the meals out. I'm sorry I am going on a bit. Who wants to hear me dribble on about how depressed, sad and alone I am feeling. Re-write. My time down in Cornwall was wild and adventurous; meeting Ross Poldark on the moors who took me by the hand to climb Brown Willy. That's the highest point on Bodmin Moor in case the reference was lost on you. When we reached the top our eyes fix intently on each other, the wild winds blow through our hair as our lips touch and we passionately embrace. I feel his bulge swell as our two bodies rub against each other. What? It could happen. My mind wonders back to real life. And then to Adam. And then to Hank, and then to Stavros. Oh, put it away Stavros.

Chapter 3

The night before

I need to confess I got a bit Glen Close last night. To justify my actions, it was day five after splitting up; if I'm still doing this after day fifty-five than let's start thinking about calling the police, but for now, let's just call it a small blip. I just couldn't sleep. I was still processing what had led to the breakup of our relationship. Questions raced through my mind, speculations on the reasoning, what Adam was thinking and what he was doing, and why hadn't he called. I then decided to download Grindr. No intention of creating a profile for me, but so I could see if Adam had started to move on. No details of me at this stage, just a completely blank profile so I can secretly observe. I set the location for where Adam lives and as the search results start to be revealed, and there he is. A little one centimetre square box of him topless, smiling away with his biceps on full display. I took that photograph when we went on holiday last year and now he's using it for hooking up with other guys! Prick. That wasn't the first thought though, when I saw the little image of the smiley person, I felt like my heart had just been ripped out and then forced back down my throat to swallow.

Frozen, I don't know what to do. I look again at Adam's profile. It reads:

Name: Fun

Age: 41 (he's not 41 he's 45)

Description: Recently Single, looking for no strings fun

Height: 5'8

Body Type: Muscular

Tribes: Jock, Clean-Cut

Relationship status: Single

Looking for: Right now, Friends, Dates

Position: Versatile

Accepts NSFW Pics: Yes

Without thinking I add him as a favourite. I re-read the description again and again and I screen shot his photos. I get he will be moving on with his life, but it's the speed at which he does that feels painful. I search for profiles in New York. Who would be Adam's type? I think New York as this is a cosmopolitan city that's bound to have loads of hot guys. He's always said he likes tall, dark and hairy guys. Was he saying that because that's me? Was that a lie? All the guys in New York are buff. I stumble across a guy in his late forties who is shirtless against a backdrop of a river. I take a screenshot with my phone and then edit it so I can upload it as me. Photo under moderation. This takes fifty minutes which is the longest fifty minutes I have ever had to wait. Eager to start chatting to Adam again I start creating my profile. Let's call him Jamie. 45, single, versatile, also looking for fun – isn't everyone on Grindr? Approved. Yes. I send my first message. It's a simple 'Hi'. My rod is cast, so to speak, and immediately there's a catch.

Fun – Wow nice profile pic.

Jamie – Thank you, you look hot too.

Fun – What are you looking for?

Jamie – Just no strings fun really.

Fun – Me too. Not long out of relationship.

(Jonathan – I know. You can probably still smell me on your bedsheets!)

Jamie – Oh really, how long you been single

for?

Fun – A few weeks.

(Jonathan – Err, liar.)

Jamie – Well I'm up for fun, what are you into?

Fun – Lots of kissing, lots of body contact, I'm versatile.

(Jonathan – Plummets to a feeling of even deeper self loathing)

Jamie – Cool I'll be up for that. I'm versatile too.

Fun – Anymore pics?

(Jonathan – Searches for a big penis.)

Jamie – Here you go.

Fun – Very impressive, here's a few of me.

(Jonathan – Bastard.)

Jamie – Very nice. You've got a great body!

Fun – Thanks, work out 5 times a week. Running and yoga too.

(Jonathan – How have you managed to get your egotistical head in that small 1cm square box?)

Jamie – I can see!

(Jonathan – Why am I doing this?)

Jamie – So how come you're single?

Fun – I felt I couldn't be myself around my ex. Started questioning everything, realised I need time to find out who I am. So that's what I'm gonna do from now. And it wasn't completely right and felt I was not prepared to settle.

(Jonathan – Do you want to just kick me a few more times in the head whilst I'm down?)

Jamie – Awww, I see. You feeling better for it now?

Fun – I'm getting there.

(Jonathan – I can see.)

Jamie – Yeah, I split with my ex 4 months ago. Just looking for fun and friends for a bit.

Fun – Well I could help with that. We could be friends with benefits.

(Jonathan – Cunt.)

Jamie – Yes, I'll be up for that. Relationships are difficult, so no strings is good.

Fun – Tell me about it. Sex is so important. My ex was intimidated by my sexuality and body.

(Jonathan – No I wasn't!)

Jamie – I wouldn't be intimidated by you. We'll be having wild sex all the time. Lol.

Fun – Sounds good to me!

Jamie – You met other guys on here?

Fun – A few.

(Jonathan – Slut.)

Jamie – You interested in threesomes? I have a mate I sometimes play with.

Fun – Yes, I'm looking to try everything. Life is too short.

(Jonathan – Life is fucking hurtful.)

Jamie – Cool. Think we could have some fun together.

Fun – You looking for now?

Jamie – Yes I'm up for now.

Fun – Can you accommodate?

(Jonathan – Yes in my mother's home in Cornwall.)

Jamie – Yes.

(Jonathan – Why did you say that?)

Fun – I could come round now. Where are you?

(Jonathan – Quickly searches Google Map for a nearby address.)

Jamie – 202 Castle Street.

Fun – You're about 15 minutes away from me. Shall I come over?

(Jonathan – Ponders.)

Jamie – Yes just need to jump in shower. Message me when you park up.

Fun – Great will do. See you in a bit.

Jamie – Perfect.

(Jonathan – Feels completely worthless.)

Fun – Parked up.

Jamie – Great, just ring the bell.

Fun – Ok.

Jamie – Block.

(Jonathan – Smiles.)

As sad and pathetic as it seems, I take comfort in the disappointment and embarrassment Adam is about to feel. I picture him knocking on the door with the expectation of being greeted by beefy Jamie from the Big Apple only to be greeted by someone else. Sorry to whoever lives at 202 Castle Street, and sorry to you Adam. You don't deserve any of this. I know deep down you cannot live your life for another person. I told you this when you were struggling with your previous partner. I just wasn't expecting this to be me now. The satisfaction I feel is only short lived. I go back to feeling alone. Alone and sad that in less than 12 hours I'd be waking up to being forty in a life I was not expecting.

I'd like to say that was the end of my stalking. That I listened to my rational self when it said that it was not healthy and I needed to move on. I can't say that. I went on to create several other profiles so I could track Adam's whereabouts. He went on to create several profiles too. I guess Jamie was not the only time waster who he'd come across. Or perhaps he was conflicted in his new single life? I'm portraying Adam as a villain which is not the case, he is not a bad person, and I expect if he wrote his account of what went on it would be a completely different story. I would be this geeky boring nerd who was too quiet, too boring, too serious. But this is my account of what happened, and at the moment I'm feeling used and cheated.

Chapter 4

Adam

It sounds corny as hell to say but it felt magical when we first met two years ago. It was at Church, which is gay slang for meeting on Grindr. We were both single, alone and bored one Saturday night and both in the bath passing the time by scrolling through profiles, something sadly I had gotten accustomed to. This had been my life for the past six months. Prior to this I had a one-year relationship with an older guy, Steve, and prior to that a fifteen-year relationship with my first boyfriend and civil partner Tom, who I met when I was twenty. At this point in my life, I was starting to feel despondent on how life was turning out. I would go on the odd first date, some turned out well, others less so, hardly any second dates, never any thirds. More of my contacts were for casual sex. This satisfied part of me, but when the guy left at the end of the night, I was left wanting more. So, when I met Adam, it felt like the universe had brought us together. Now I just think how mistaken I was. Sorry, must be positive.

We actually 'met' about three weeks before. Virtually anyway. We had started talking online and I suggested going on a dog walk at the weekend which he agreed too. Then two days before we were due to meet Adam's profile and all of the messages had disappeared. Vanished. I was not sure if I had been blocked or whether Adam had just deleted his profile, but despite this I found myself chatting again to the same hot guy one Saturday night and we clicked ...

Adam suggests he comes round for a coffee. 'What are we doing at home on a Saturday night, we should meet up?'

I agree thinking he will not show based on our previous exchange a few weeks ago, but I give my address and then stay in the bath longer thinking I won't hear from him again.

My phone pings, 'Leaving now.' Shit. I quickly

get out of the bath and put on some clothes. Tight fitting t-shirt, tick, skinny jeans, tick, best pants, tick. I've been going to the gym so have been feeling more confident about my body. I'm still no Muscle Mary. That's a very odd term, isn't it? How many Marys do you know who are muscular? I wonder how the Marys in this world feel about that phrase? It's like the Susans. I feel sorry for them too, even if they are lazy cows. Anyway, you would describe me as toned rather than muscular and despite the number of hours I've been putting in, it does not change dramatically, but it is enough to feel good about myself. Adam arrives.

There is an instant bond which neither of us have ever really felt before. Chemistry, you could say. He smelt amazing too, Tom Ford Leather which soon becomes his associated scent. Adam completely adored Raff and was happy sitting on the sofa with him lapping up all the attention whilst the two of us swapped relationship scars and war stories. I think we were both at transitional stages in our lives. We had both come out of long-term relationships, Adam's much more recent and he was still living with his ex whilst they were selling their house. We both shared a pursuit for a healthy lifestyle, but did not like actual sports, except fitness and the gym. More importantly we shared the same open mindset to life. Despite this connection, I questioned how Adam must be feeling and was confident I would be placed in the friend's zone. Which was okay, Adam seemed a nice, genuine guy and someone who would make a good addition to my life in whatever capacity.

Adam had other ideas after his second coffee. I stood up looking for snacks. He walked up to me and approached to kiss. I was taken aback to say the least. What did he see in me? Here was a gorgeous, chiselled jaw, six pack, bulging-muscled guy wanting to kiss me. We did kiss and it felt great. We looked sheepishly into each other's eyes afterwards before returning for more. I had dated other guys, I'd been in two serious relationships, but I had never felt the excitement as I did in that moment. We continued to talk, interlaced with kissing until we found our way to my bedroom. I felt nervous. I'm usually confident when it comes to sex. Despite my body hang ups I can enjoy the moment and get down and dirty like the next guy. My experience with Adam was different. Touching his defined chest and six pack as we had sex was unbelievable. At one point in the night I asked him if he was really a male hooker sent by my friends who all had a whip round for him to cheer me up. To which he laughed and said that was the kindest insult he had been given. But that's how I felt, disbelief that he was attracted to me, and that all my Christmases had come at once. I had to pinch myself that he was there. He had arrived in my life at the right time. Or so I thought.

In hindsight, I wonder now how much of my feelings were based on flattery that someone like Adam would want to be with me. I later questioned if it was really the right time. Was Adam ready for a relationship? Being completely honest he was not really my type physically. I could appreciate his body, and this I did over the two years we dated, but my type would probably be older, taller, hairier. Adam was smooth (apart from his hairy arse) but over time I grew to love that body of his. And I miss it now. I bet Hank is enjoying his body.

It was an intense night where we stayed up until 4 am. Talking, having sex, having more sex, talking and then more sex. I learnt all about his childhood, his past relationships, his lost dreams and his future ones. I think Adam was my first true love where I experienced the butterflies in my stomach. I've never been one for public displays of affection, and never a hand holder, but I wanted to hold Adam's hand in public all the time. I was proud that he was with me, and I wanted everyone to know about it. That morning we woke in each other's arm. The sun beamed strongly and there was a freshness in the air that I had never noticed before. It felt like I was the lead in my very own Rom-Com.

The weeks that followed we spent a lot of time together. Basically, all the time. We met the next day for a drink in a beer garden at a local pub. There we continued to talk and learn of our connection with each other. Things were perfect. Adam only lived about two miles away. He was living with his ex at the time whilst they completed a renovation on their house and then later sold it. He spent more time with me and Raff in my flat than he did his own. We would often meet at the gym, do a workout together than he would end up staying back at mine. Very early on we carved out this arrangement. I went along with it despite liking, no needing, my own space, but we were happy. I soon missed the rare nights when he was not with me. This was a good time in our relationship. I was in love.

The sex was great. I say sex rather than making love as most of the time that's what it felt like. One time, on our many breaks up and the analysis of what had gone wrong as we often did, I told Adam that it felt like we had first time sex the whole time. This was not meant to be a criticism, although at the time this is how he perceived it, in fact it was the opposite, there was passion in how we made love. I'm using the words making love now. But we never looked each other in the eyes. When I became aware of this I tried to initiate it but Adam would not always respond. Thinking about it, that must mean it was more Adam's issue as it was mine, right? When we later got back together, a week on from that conversation, we both looked attentively in each other's eyes whilst we had sex. It's sex again now. This continued for about a week until it returned back to what we had before. I guess there were cracks in the relationship almost from the offset. I think we both ignored these as the pull of being together was so much stronger than not being together. That pull is still there. I question if Adam feels the same too. See, I'm questioning again.

My Top 20 moments with Adam (it was going to be 10 but I could not narrow it down!)

I'm a massive fan of lists so here we go:

1. Being dressed as ninja bunnies hopping around the estate at midnight as we hide easter eggs for a neighbourhood easter egg hunt that we did as a surprise for everyone.

2. Going to Pride for the first time as we walked around holding hands.

3. Going skinny dipping on a cold November early morning in Cornwall (my idea) whilst Raff looked on with a look in his eyes as if to say what the fuck are they doing?

4. Just holding hands as we watched TV together – we did this a lot.

5. Educating each other on classic films – Adam introduced me to The Lost Boys, 2001 Space Odyssey and Poltergeist whilst I shared Curly Sue, Mean Girls and Out of

Africa. We both cried like babies at the end of that one.

6. Going to the gym together where Adam would make me work that little bit harder and I would always get stroppy and come up with an excuse as to why I could not do it.

7. Walking in a packed high street holding hands and catching a lady's eye who smiles back.

8. The breakfasts we shared in the morning – we always had amazing breakfasts whilst listening to the news on the radio.

9. Whilst on holiday, Adam holding my hair back as I vomited profusely, still completely drunk and laughing hilariously at the fact that I challenged a professional dancer to a dance-off and won. My interpretation anyway.

10. Taking a cycle ride with Raff in a bike trailer we bought – Raff absolutely loved it. Even though he was being pulled along (like royalty) he was so shattered that evening.

11. Seeing Adam pick a shard of glass from Raff's paw and giving him a big kiss on his head as if he was his own new-born baby – oh my god he adored Raff and must miss him so much.

12. Cooking amazing dinners whilst chatting

over wine – we became quite creative you know. I think Adam thought he was a bit of a Jamie Oliver. His ex had tended to do the cooking and said Adam couldn't be trusted to do it so he loved the freedom and expression of cooking for us. Although one time he did put Greek Yogurt in the sweet potato mash. It tasted pretty bad.

13. Star gazing – we were both fascinated by astrology. I would often try and contemplate the size of the planets, the universe, and the galaxy. It gives you a real perspective on life, don't you think?

14. Going to a concert for the first time.

15. Adam reading a chapter a night of the book The Silver Sword, a book from my childhood. We never did finish that book.

16. Just going on long dog walks, packing a flask of tea, some water for Raff and a few dog chews for a pit stop.

17. My first time going camping. I was too tall for the tent and had my feet pressed up against the sides leading to wet socks from a pool of condensation the next morning. A favourite moment, but never again.

18. Adam eating someone else's breakfast one time. We were in a packed beer garden for brunch and little known to us someone had sat at our table, ordered food, and then

moved to a sunnier spot. Then whilst I was ordering food from the bar, the other person's teacake and coffee arrived. Adam thought I had ordered it as a pre brunch snack and had already consumed one half and was spreading marmalade on the other as I returned. 'What are you doing? Where did you get that from?' 'You ordered it.' 'Errrr, no'. We looked around and could see the mistake, the woman's face as she saw Adam devouring her teacake. I still get belly laughs now as I think about that.

19. Going on an Egyptian Cruise and seeing Adam so fascinated as we woke in the Suez Canal, his eyes fixated to the new world around him and I saw him as a seven year old child peering through the ships window mesmerised by what he was seeing and feeling.

20. The first night we met.

I often think that if we lived on a desert island with no one around, well apart from Raff, then our relationship would have survived and we would have lived happily ever after. But life is not an island. We live in a world with other people, other priorities, baggage and insecurities which slowly crept into being. There was a period of time where I was happy to ignore these cracks and focus on the end point. I recently learnt of the Japanese art of

Kintsugi. It involves putting broken pottery back together using gold as a way of symbolising that something can be stronger by being rebuilt and embracing the flaws and imperfections. I thought this must be the case for us. That we were learning through our break ups and like that piece of pottery were bonded by gold. In my mind I could picture us living in a beautiful house, perhaps back in Cornwall. We would take long walks on the beach, chat over morning breakfast, go running, enjoy holidays, just be. I'll explain more about those cracks a bit later on but I think one of them was around communication. I don't think this was Adam's dream. I was not his dream, but for whatever reason he could not say this to me until last week.

I start to question though how much my body at that point was telling me that things were not right. I would always describe myself as an intuitive person and would often pick up on his feelings. I think I was hearing his conflict at times, and my reaction was to shut down. That sounds like a bit of a cop out, I know. Let me explain as I'm not one for blaming others for how I feel. I have an internal locus of control. I get annoyed (well marginally, annoyed might be too strong a word) when I hear other's say, 'he made me feel sad.' No, you felt sad because he dumped you. The action can be owned by the other person, the feeling you have is owned by you. Of course, this still means you feel sad, but it helps to know that this is within our control. Towards the end of our relationship, if I'm being honest, I was doubting if he did want that life with me, or a fresh start.

This chapter was meant to focus on our good times. I can recognise that there were many of these. I've deleted most of his photos from my phone now but as I was doing this there was what seemed a picture-perfect relationship. I think this is where my struggle comes from, and my inability to let go. We almost made this work.

***

It's only been two weeks since we split and I still think of Adam a zillion times a day. To be expected, I guess? Friends tell me that it will get easier, but when exactly? I messaged him today. I tried to be really good and resist the urge, but I couldn't stop myself. The exchange was good, he told me that he still misses me. That he feels lost too. We agreed to give it more time. Time for what exactly? What I want most is just to be close to him, for our bodies to be intertwined as one and feel his beating chest against mine as we lie in bed and pretend everything is okay. I do realise that would be a lie, but that's allowed for just a few hours right?

Chapter 5

Time's a healer (apparently)

Nearly two months after our split I feel that I have not moved on. On a daily, no hourly basis I will track Adam's movement. I know the exact location of where he lives, sandwiched between the profile names 'Straightish' – I know, you're on Grindr, you're not straight – and 'Balloon Fetish', who knew but apparently it's a thing. I would know where in the county Adam was for work. Occasionally I would see Adam move, three squares down, two across. This I knew was when he was meeting other guys. It was torture and I have no idea why I put myself through this.

I would masturbate to the thought of Adam which was odd as I never did that within our relationship or whilst on the numerous breaks we had. Is that normal? Not the obsession bit, I know that's not normal, but do couples masturbate thinking of their partner? Or was that just one on the number of cracks which were there at the start of ours? I wonder if Adam used to jerk off thinking about me? I would be surprised if he did. Too busy jerking off thinking about himself.

I would also send him regular texts, but rather than send them to him, I would send them to me. Just little every day, thinking about you type messages.

Jonathan – Hi, hope you are having a good day. Still think about you.

Jonathan – Hey, how are you doing? All good here, busy, busy with work. Do you want to meet up soon?

Jonathan – Morning, thought I would just send you a message to say hey. Hope you have a good day.

Jonathan – Just one more day until the weekend! Anything planned? I'm just having a quiet one here. Anyhow hope you are well?

Unsurprisingly, when I received these messages back, I just felt pathetic. Occasionally I did send Adam a message to his actual phone along the lines of above. I would do this periodically until I realised I was always the one who sent the first message, and always the one who sent the last. I therefore thought why bother, and to try and maintain the little dignity I had, I stopped contact.

When I stopped contacting him, he started to text me. It was all about the same subject in how we were struggling to move on and a light anecdote within this. 'Raff's just rolled in a dead bird', 'Spider baby (a plant I grew) is getting huge', 'Saw Steve, he said "hi"'. One group of messages started to get quite flirtatious. By this point I had only had sex once in two months so was feeling horny. I would have, but Adam, rightfully so suggested it was not a good idea. Then things fizzled out further. We said when we split we would have some distance but remain friends. This remaining friends turned out to be difficult. I wanted us to help each other as we both knew what the other was going through, but helping Adam was at the cost of helping myself and I think this was the same for him.

There were times when it felt he was looking for an excuse to hate me and misconstrued what I was saying, this ended in him blocking my number. Strangely the anger I felt towards this action made it easier for me to move on, mildly easier anyway. Actually, I'm not sure if it was easier at all.

At this point it's fair to say I reached a new low. I was a human doing, rather than a human being. I didn't tell anyone at work that we had split, instead making an excuse for any invites we had to go out. I still functioned, but everything felt foggy. I would brush my teeth in the mornings until they bled. I took comfort spitting out blood. I don't really know why this was. Was it a reminder that I was alive? Did I see this as a way of self-punishment. I ate very little, drank a lot, smoked even more. When I did eat it was standing up as I couldn't face sitting at the dining table alone. I loved music but hadn't realised that so many songs on the radio were about love. I resorted to listening to 80s music instead as this was the only genre I could stomach. Work and Raff structured my day. There was little else in between.

When I wasn't feeling sad, I was angry with the world. Minor occurrences which ordinarily I wouldn't even notice or care sent me into a spin. The almond croissant which was dry, the morning traffic, the yucky mummy who couldn't park her oversized 4x4, which I swear she had to get due to her enormous arse. Stupid cow. I could go on, couples holding hands in the street looking all smug and in love. I didn't feel part of this world. Correction, I didn't want to feel part of this world.

Right, make a list of Adam's bad points, it

might cheer you up:

1. He had a hairy arse.
2. He drove like an old lady.
3. He didn't want to be with me.
4. I can't do this; it's not helping me move on.

There was a period of about three weeks where Adam's profile was nowhere to be seen. I wondered why this was the case. I concluded the options were:

1. Adam has met someone and they are now having wild passionate sex, perhaps a cushion fight where all the feathers explode creating a snow globe effect whilst they are on the bed.
2. Adam has now met so many guys he has their numbers so can direct message them. He has men for each night of the week who visit and pleasure him. Hank on a Monday, Stavros on a Tuesday, Marco Wednesdays, etc etc.
3. Adam has caught on to the fact that he is being followed and upgraded his account to Incognito mode which allows him to still chat to other guys but will be invisible for everybody else on there.
4. Adam is struggling too and gave up hope on finding people through Grindr.

None of these options were favourable to me. Well, perhaps the last one if I'm being honest.

We do meet up. He brings over a bag full of Raff's things – basket, food bowl, kibbles, toys and treats. I make him a coffee and think how well he is looking. He has lost weight too. He too is struggling, apparently, as he talks about the sadness he is feeling.

'It's what you wanted though, you initiated this,' I responded.

'I just want to be loved.'

'You were loved,' I reply.

'Yes, but I felt uncomfortable a lot of the times. I couldn't cope with your silences. And I want a relationship where we make love, not just have sex.'

I can't hear this. I feel a barrier coming up. Even though it is an observation I had previously made, hearing it in this way is just a little too real for me. It validates my insecurities that I was not enough. Before he leaves, he looks at me as if he is toying with kissing me. I can see the apprehension in his eyes.

'I do love you,' he says.

'Yes, but is that enough?'

We hug. He looks longingly at me again, as if he's working out whether to kiss me or not. He doesn't. He leaves, and the door is closed once again. This time for the final time.

The weeks continue much in the same vein. I know I'm going on a bit. I'm just trying to portray the impact this has had on me. I feel tired. That's a severe understatement. For all this time I have carried this burden of loving someone who no longer loves me back. Or even if at some level he does still love me, I'm being told I'm not enough. I've watched him move on with his life, I was there at every step of the blossoming relationship with Stavros; their first kiss, when they made love, the first time Adam made him a coffee in bed, the first morning after breakfast they shared (it was scrambled eggs and smoked salmon) the night they stayed up until four sharing childhood stories, relationship break-ups and their inner most thoughts and feelings. I had been replaced and was now one of his breakup stories he was telling Stavros about.

Having your head filled with these thoughts is wearing. On top of this, I pushed my body to an inch of its life. Yoga every morning, two-hour gym sessions, not standing still. A desperation to improve my image in an attempt to gain the confidence that I had lost. Even when I stopped for a cigarette I was doing butt clenches. I kept busy as I was worried about what would happen when I stopped.

Slowly though things did improve, slightly. I was surprised to realise at the gym that I hadn't thought of Adam for thirty minutes. And these gaps started to increase. I have good days and bad days. I still regularly check my phone for messages and his whereabouts, but less frequently, and I've started to think about meeting other people.

Chapter 6

Butterfly

To move on I realise I need to make some changes to my life, starting with the exterior. As cliché as it sounds, I start with a haircut. For a while I had been thinking of going silver grey. At forty grey is starting to appear in my hair and beard anyway and I thought this would be sophistication. Something different. I contemplated going to the hairdressers but decided this was within my capabilities. Wrong. I later learn that watching

YouTube videos does not make you the next hairstylist to the stars. With naturally dark hair, I buy a blonde set to strip the colour, then the silver one to follow. How easy. This is going to look amazing, I tell myself. As you can see, I'm very excited about this.

The blonde goes on. It should take thirty minutes. As I have very dark hair, though, I leave it in for forty-five. Has it taken? It's hard to say. After another ten minutes, as my scalp starts to burn, I decide that it is long enough so set about rinsing and washing it out. As I look up at the mirror I'm greeted by a straw yellow. I could be one of the Simpsons at this point. I get a sinking feeling in my gut. Oh fuck. I stare intently and cannot help but laugh. Okay, well that's not the final look. There is the silver to add, which has a strange purple tint to the dye. Thirty minutes becomes forty, becomes fifty and I wash it out again. I look in the mirror. I think maybe I should get another mirror, or just banish them all entirely as it has not taken and instead it's made my hair look even more blond. At least it is not yellow anymore and it is different which is what I wanted. It does look shocking though, and I'm not sure it's the height of sophistication I was going for.

With the real danger of my hair falling out I wear a hat for the entire week as I cannot risk adding anymore colour. People assume it's a fashion thing where I'm sporting a new cosmopolitan look, but really I'm hiding the disaster on top of my head. Then once a week has passed, I go back to my natural brown hair which by now feels like straw, but it's just about salvageable to pass off as my own. It's the UK, people are too polite to comment. I do have to contend with some staring though. Note to self, don't mess with hair again. Ever.

I don't stop here. I book a consultation with an Aesthetician. I spend days googling various treatment options before deciding on Botox on my forehead and filler on my cheeks and in my lips. I don't want some great trout pout, but I look at my lips and see no volume or anything. I mean, it doesn't stop me being a good kisser, but I just feel it will help my confidence. Three days later I'm speaking to the lovely Matt on what feels like a dentist's chair, but this one is purple and has no little sink which you spit into. He agrees with my choice of treatments and tells me the Botox is prescription only so I need to come back for that, but he can do the filler there and then. 'Why not,' I reply.

It's an odd sensation. It doesn't hurt, it's just a bit of discomfort, I guess, and this strange crackling sensation I can feel and hear under the skin. I know this isn't going to transform my life, but it gives me the foundations where I feel good about myself so I can start the more meaningful steps which will make a difference. The procedure itself takes ten minutes and I see myself looking back at me in the mirror more fresh-faced and almost line free. A week later I'm back for the Botox which is an even quicker and simpler procedure. It's a few days before I see the effects of this and I'm left feeling fresh, new and rejuvenated and thankfully not sporting an almond shaped face like some people do.

I go shopping and max out my credit card, on, well everything. I go for different looks. Who am I trying to be? A more stylish, fashionable, hip, trendy Jonathan. An 'I don't care what people think of me' Jonathan. Which is ironic as I'm making more of an effort on my appearance so clearly I do care. I don't care what they cost though. Who needs savings? I was planning a trip to New York for Adam's birthday and put some money aside for that. Well that isn't happening now so I may as well use the money to look good. I did look good. I didn't really feel good though. Well, that exchange at the till felt good. Trying them on felt good. Carrying the shiny bags with my new possessions felt good. Then I got home and thought I had nowhere to wear them. That needed to be my next focus. Perhaps that should have been my first focus, oh well I've brought them now.

I take this further and buy a new car. Again, why do I need my savings? I'm no longer going to be buying a big dream house with Adam. My flat is more than sufficient for Raff and me. It did feel good walking around the Mercedes dealership. I felt good then. I felt confident. As I drove home in my brand new Merc I felt elevated to a new status. Again, this feeling did not last long and I was stuck with the huge monthly payments which equalled my mortgage. Jonathan, look up the meaning of being sensible.

The car was primarily only used to go to the gym. A lot. This became my new focus. Everyday; two hours of gym sessions. I was intimidated to go into the free weight area at first. Adam used to set everything up and I would only go when he was there, but over time the gym became a sanctuary to me and I worked hard. I had lost weight from the split, not that I needed to, I was always slim, but my stomach where I carried the small weight I had was as flat as it ever had been. I used this as a catalyst to improve further. I pretty much lived on salmon and broccoli. I think I alone may be responsible for the decline in fishing stocks. I was looking good for it though.

I go to the dentist, I decide to get great big brilliant white veneers. I've always been conscious of my smile. No one has said anything when I've made reference to them, but I've had small gappy teeth. Little baby teeth I would think. I want a Hollywood smile, even if I have little to smile about. I first set about whitening the teeth. 'Build it up gradually, just put it on for an hour or so as it can lead to sensitivity.' Straight away I leave it on overnight. Every night. Until I'm left with a white that is probably a tad artificial and one that would attract moths on a dark night. Then once whitened I go back for the veneers. It was pain free and took no longer than three hours and at the end of it I was blown away.

'Oh wow'. 'These are probably one of my best works, the transformation is amazing. Now they can take a bit of getting used to. Can you say fish fingers?'

I reply, 'eish eengers.' Where have my F's gone? I try again. 'Eish eengers.' The dentist's assistant looks embarrassed as I cannot talk.

'Keep practicing and it will get better.' That drive home I practice my alphabet. It took just over a week for my speech to return to normal, but I didn't care, I looked ucking amazing!

Once I get my F's back and am able to string a sentence together I decide to get some professional photographs taken and show off my new killer smile and the body I had been working so hard for. A friend, Chris, (more on him later but he is a guy I met online and developed a good friendship with where we both connected in the harsh realities of being forty, single and gay) told me that 'I'm much better looking in person than in photos!' I think there is a compliment in there somewhere. He suggests I get some professionally done. His ex does photography so Chris suggests I contact him, which I bravely do, and now Mark is in my living room with his camera as we agree on six or seven different outfits to wear and a few more risqué shirtless ones. At first, I'm nervous as hell as I sit, stand, lean and arch my body into different positions to the sound of the clicking of the camera. Mark was great though and really put me at ease. 'I think you can undo a couple more buttons,' he confidently said. So, I did, and revealed my broad slightly hairy chest. It felt great.

In fact, I found Mark with his camera pressed to his face a little bit sexy but ruled out dating friend's exes, even if my friendship with Chris was only a few weeks old, so just discounted this motion immediately. Bros before hoes and all that. I reflected on Chris and Mark's past relationship and wondered what had gone wrong. I knew Chris's account but not Mark's and I did think physically they seemed suited to each other. But people often said Adam and I were suited and were surprised when we split. Towards the end of the photo shoot, I really got into it. Raff joined in for a few shots and I was left with an array of natural and posed pictures, all ready for my next steps in getting back out there and dating again.

That night I dreamt about Mark. It's odd I rarely remember my dreams. I think we were just hanging out and we started holding hands as we watched TV. That's what Adam and I would do. Was there something in Mark that reminded me of Adam, or Tom even, my first relationship from twenty years ago? Mark seemed quite introverted like me which I found endearing and not in your face like Adam was. He would jump around like the Duracell Bunny. I think it may have been nervous energy. I found this cute at first but if I'm being honest after a while this started to get on my nerves. It was like our relationship was too much of him and not about us. I'm only starting to see this now. People are funny. The subconscious is funny. Anyway, thinking about Mark was a welcome break from thinking of Adam.

Chapter 7

MOT

I decide it is probably a good time to get tested before putting myself out there in the new dating world. It has been a while since I last had STI tests and before I move on with that aspect of my life, I want to make sure that I'm carrying no nasty bugs, or whatever viruses are. During the numerous splits in my relationship with Adam, I had the odd one-night stand so I'm definitely right to get tested.

Googling the local GUM clinic nearest to me I see the opening times for drop-in sessions. That's easier, I think. I will just get up super early, be one of the first to be seen then I'll be back home within an hour, simples. The only problem is that everyone has this idea too. As I approach the clinic, I'm greeted by a line of ten people already waiting outside and the building does not open for another twenty minutes. There is no stigma in getting tested, more people need to do it, but I did still feel a bit ashamed as I wait in line, very self-consciously, not daring to make eye contact with anyone, worried a work colleague or acquaintance will pass whilst I'm queuing.

As I wait, others join. Most of the people appear to be gay men. I know I'm making sweeping assumptions here and I do not mean to suggest that gay men are more promiscuous. In fact, I've just come back from a dog walk with Steve and he was telling me all about a single heterosexual friend he knows who has just joined dating sites aimed at hook ups rather than dates and has been inundated with requests for sex and threesomes and to be tied up and beaten by this woman and her two female friends. So, these days everyone is at it. Anyway, I digress again, I recognise a few guys from their Grindr profile, who account for the main demographic other than the odd teenage girl who waits for the morning-after-pill. In fact, I recognise one of the guys from a sexual encounter I had over three years ago, then another. God, does that make me a slut? Don't answer that God, I'll direct that question to someone with looser morals.

As they open the doors, we all shuffle in huddled together like penguins. I'm given a clip board and pen and asked to complete the form and return to reception. Right, need to act quickly. This is where I can make up time by being one of the first to be seen. I quickly answer the questions – name, age, date of birth, address, time since last attending, what contacts I've had and the questions go on and on. I'm disadvantaged by the pen I have been given where the ink has started to dry, just write damn you, write I shout in my head. That adds at least two minutes to my time and I see several people complete their forms before me. Bastards. I do complete it though, hand it to reception and diligently wait.

After an hour my name is called. This felt like a long hour as I really needed the toilet but I'd read about the screenings and that a urine sample is needed for the first one. During this time everyone is quiet and no one makes eye contact. Most have their heads down and are on their phones. I wonder how many of them are on Grindr or any other dating platforms? No, that can't be right. No one would try and hook up in a GUM clinic surely? I follow the Nurse to a small examination room where I'm asked to take a seat.

'Can you confirm your name and date of birth?' I confirm my name and date of birth.

'And can you just confirm your address for me please?' I confirm my address for her. I feel like a twelve-year-old in the headmaster's office. Not that I was there much, I was a good boy at school.

'I can see from the form you are wanting full screening.'

'Yes, that's right.'

'And you are a gay male?'

'Yes, I am a gay male.'

'We just need to take some history of your last sexual contacts.'

'Okay,' I reply.

'How many sexual partners have you had in the past three months?'

'Two people,' I explain.

'And did that include oral sex?'

'Yes.'

'Is that giving or receiving or both?'

'Both.'

'And was that with a condom?'

'No, it was not.'

'That's okay, no one does,' she replies.

'And anal sex?'

'Yes and anal sex.'

'And was that giving or receiving or both?'

'It was both.'

'And was that wearing condoms?'

'No, not with my long-term partner but the

other guy, yes.'

'And do you have any symptoms or concerns,' the Nurse asks.

'No, no symptoms, I have recently split from my partner so thought now would be a good time to get checked out.'

'Yes, it is. And have you paid for sex?'

'What? No.'

'Okay, sorry it's a question we have to ask. And would you like to take some free condoms.'

'Oh, it's okay.'

'Go on they're free.'

'No, it's fine'.

'Are you sure?'

'Yes, I'm sure.'

The Nurse, who I can see from her name badge is called Carol, seems disappointed from my refusal as if she is on commission. She then tells me what to expect. I'm given two swabs, one for my throat and one for my rectum. Her words, I would have just said this goes up your bum. I'm also given a small pot to pee in. They are labelled. I'm then told to go into Toilet B and then once I'm done to post them in the box adjacent to the toilets. Gosh it's all carefully planned, I think.

'Then take a seat and we will call you again for your bloods. We will be doing tests for Chlamydia, Gonorrhoea, Trichomoniasis, HIV, Syphilis and Hepatitis B.

'Okay,' I reply.

'Toilet B' the Nurse informs me again. She's nice but quite forceful. A bit old school matron like.

In Toilet B, I carry out my tests. I won't go into detail but you can guess where they all go as the Nurse described them above. I then post them and return to the same seat where I was sitting before. A further twenty-minute wait and I'm called again to have my blood taken by a different nurse.

'Could you confirm your name and date of birth.' I confirm my name and date of birth.

'And could you confirm your address. I confirm my address.

'So, we are going to take some bloods from you. If you can roll up your sleeve, are you left or right-handed?'

'Right.'

'Let's take it from the left then, are you okay with bloods?'

'Yes, I don't like to see it come out, but I will be fine.'

The Nurse hunts for a vein and in her second attempt takes two small pots of blood.

I feel slight light-headedness but I've got this.

'All done, that wasn't too bad was it?'

'No,' I reply.

'Have you been offered any condoms, before you go?'

'Yes, the other Nurse offered. It's okay I'm

okay for condoms.'

'Are you sure, they are free?'

'Oh go on then yes I'll have some condoms.'

I take a small paper bag of condoms and leave. I swear if I didn't take them I think she would have snuck them in my coat pocket whilst I was not looking. I'm told that results will be ten days or so and I will be contacted. I leave, again head down in fear of making eye contact.

It was nine days later when I get a call from the clinic. I've tested positive for Gonorrhoea. I'm told to return to have an injection of antibiotics and then made another appointment for further re-tests to make sure it has worked. I'm told to inform all sexual partners of this result. This isn't going to be awkward. Of course, I'm being facetious here.

I ponder who I caught it from. Was it from Adam? I google symptoms of Gonorrhoea. I don't recall a time when I experienced any of those. How long have I had it for? I'm secretly pleased as it is a reason to contact him. I text immediately.

Jonathan – Hi, hope you are okay? Can we talk later?

Three hours later and there is no reply. I know he has his phone on him as I'm still stalking him on Grindr. I send another message.

Jonathan - Hey, just to add it's nothing major in case you are worried that I'm going to be in tears again or wanting a heavy conversation about us but ideally something I would rather talk than message (just in case your delay in replying is because you were anxious about what it is all about).

Two hours later and still no reply.

Jonathan – Are you getting these messages? A simple, yeah let's talk later will be good.

Adam – Sorry, really busy day. I'll be home in an hour if you want to talk then.

Adam called as he said he would. 'Is everything alright?'

'Yeah hang on, I'm just in the hall, I was about to go out with Raff.'

'Okay, can you not walk and talk?'

'No, I don't want my neighbours hearing this conversation'.

Now back in my flat the conversation continues.

'I wanted to talk to you about something, I went to get STI tests, not because I have any symptoms or anything but because I just thought it would be a good time to do it. The results came back today and I have Gonorrhoea.'

A pause. 'Oh right, I see, okay. Guess I had better get tested too then?'

The conversation continued. 'Yes that's probably a good idea. So how have you been?'

'Terrible,' replies Adam. 'I don't think I've moved on at all.'

'Really?' I ask. In a strange way I'm relieved.

Despite the realisation starting to filter in that we did not have the picture-perfect relationship we once thought, or convinced ourselves that we had, we still had something and I still feel saddened by the loss of it. Hearing that Adam was finding it difficult validated my feelings of loss. Although there was still a contradiction in what he was saying to me, and how he had been behaving. I guess that may just be his way of dealing with it? To focus on the future rather than the past? Leaves me feeling crap though.

We speak for about twenty minutes in total. Nothing's changed. We still know we have to move on and it would be too much for us to remain as friends at this stage, but this phone call which I had been dreading, turned out to be a good one. When the call was ended, I let out a smile; partly that I felt connected again, partly that I knew what we had was real, but mostly because I knew Adam wouldn't be having sex for the next 10 days.

***

Three days later I'm back at the clinic for my injection. The same process awaits where I'm asked to go into detail about my sexual encounters. They have this information, I think. This time though I'm being questioned by one of the male doctors. I don't know why but this threw me and I found it strange talking to him about gay sex. He was from Nigeria I think, and although incredibly polite and gentle with his demeanour, I didn't want to be sitting there.

He explained that before they give me the injection for treatment, they need to take a further sample to test the culture or something. I don't remember exact details as I wasn't really listening. I expect Adam would say my barrier was up. Rather than a swab, however, he had to use this device thing to take a deeper sample. It looked like a plastic gun. He was searching this drawer which had multiples of this device but he seemed to be looking for a bigger one. The small one looked fine I thought in my head but I dare not question the good doctor.

'Now go behind the curtain and lower your pants and lie on the bed facing the wall.'

I'm still only half listening and think he says take off your clothes and face the wall. Thankfully I question this. 'You want me naked?' I ask.

At this stage the panicked doctor clarifies, 'no just lower.' He almost sniggered as he did. 'Now is it okay if a trainee doctor watches for practice?' There's a pause. 'You can say no.'

'No, it's fine, I'm okay with that,' I say as I lie on the bed. The next minute I hear several voices behind the screen.

'Hi, I'm Michelle one of the trainee doctors, I'm here with Emma who is also training.'

'And I'm Claire, hope it's okay if I watch too?'

'Oh great,' I cynically reply, 'no that's fine.'

I picture them all huddled together looking at my bum hole. One that I did wipe but not properly wash, or the term douched used in the gay world, as I wasn't expecting this. Perhaps a swab which I'd administer myself but not a formal occasion like this. I felt the event really needed a member of the royal family to officiate this further.

The doctor tells me he is going to apply some lube. This is so weird, I think. Then he's going to insert whatever it was called, again stopped listening at this point. 'You may feel it go in' he proudly announces. I don't but feel I should display some discomfort as I don't want him to think I'm loose, so I make the odd 'ouch' sound. I feel a small pinch and it's done.

The doctor then asks if it's okay for one of the trainees to do the procedure again. I flatly refuse 'no'. I'm then thanked by my public as they go, leaving me to pull up my pants before joining the doctor the other side of the screen.

'Was that okay?' the doctor asks.

'It felt a bit painful but was fine.' It didn't but again I wanted to keep up the pretence. I'm finally given the injection, some thick fluid which you can feel go in, but again does not hurt. Think I must have a high pain threshold. I'm told to complete a further test in two weeks, and then once this is back, I can have sex.

Jokes and embarrassment aside, living in the UK we are lucky to have this available to us. We take healthcare for granted which is not available to all. I don't know the long-term effects of Gonorrhoea but I'm guessing they are not good. I'm relieved when I hear that it has been treated, and disappointed when Adam tells me a week later that he is clear.

Chapter 8

Grindr

With a clean bill of health and newfound confidence from an image upgrade (well apart from the hair), I decide it's time to start dating again. Although still very ambiguous about it, and still thinking of Adam a lot, I delete my blank profile which I had been using to track his whereabouts and set up a proper one. It is approaching three months since we split, although it only feels like three weeks. I know, however, I cannot live my life vicariously through a blank profile. Between the app and my imagination, this current life is a window into Adam's bedroom, which is a constant drain on my self-esteem and worth. Torture, just utter torture, which I have been putting myself through.

Talking of torture, I experience Grindr in the same way. Why is everyone so aggressive on it? When I first log in, I'm greeted by an array of blank profiles. Now I would love to say that these blank images are a political statement that the guys do not want to be objectified by an image alone as a way of meeting someone and they want their personality rather than their look be their key feature. I cannot, however, say this. I learn a lot of these are married guys, closeted guys or just complete time wasters. A lot are what's called 'pic collectors'. Fucking losers is a better one.

This app is immediate. Within minutes, seconds, you can search for men around you. Although badged as a dating site, in reality it is a hook up site. Don't get me wrong, not everyone on there is like that, but in my initial experience it is the majority.

There are some genuine people on there looking for dates, friends and relationships, but the power of seeing who at the click of a button is near-by is, whilst liberating and amazing, has created a culture of immediate gratification and some people just being fucking rude. When you add to this most people are sexually charged, and rather than having a wank, which would have happened before the days of Grindr, people look for a fuck instead. This motivation brings out the worse in people.

I'm new blood. I receive countless numbers of requests for photographs of my dick. Not, 'hello great profile. Sorry to hear you are recently single. I'm Howard and I'm single too'. Just, 'More pics', or 'You hung?', or 'Dick pics.' I mean, at what point in real life would it be acceptable to act in this way, to approach somebody in a pub and ask the person to flop out their cock? Yet we are in a world where this has become the norm. When not being asked for dick pics I'm questioned on what I want. It feels like I'm being attacked most of the time from a masked mugger. 'What you looking for?' Or 'Into?' That's another common phrase, well not even a phrase, a word. There is rarely politeness, no manners, no pleasantries just a focus on instant sex.

The demographic of guys is younger than me so I struggle with finding guys to message. I prefer slightly older men and these appear to be limited. Perhaps I'm on the wrong site? Is there another one for older gay men, and at forty is this now what I have become?

I would have been a Twink in my youth. This is gay slang for a young-looking gay guy. My body shape is changing from the hours I have been putting into it, but I don't think I'm a Jock yet. I would rather undersell myself and then be a pleasant surprise. I'm a bit hairy, but slender so I'm not a Bear or a Cub. I once stroked a Bear. I'm also not Clean-Cut as a result of my facial hair. What am I? A retired Twink? I learn I'm an Otter. An Otter, how fucking boring is that? My mind moves to thinking of Otters for a bit. For many years I worked in a café at a local wildlife sanctuary in Cornwall which overlooked the Otter enclosure. I think it was called Otter Pool café come to think about it. Otters can be aggressive. Humm maybe that sums me up? I consider searching for Adam to see whether he is online. I do not do it. He's a Jock, I think. Actually no, he's a cock.

I quickly learn that not everyone is who they say they are. This should not be a complete surprise as for the past three months I have been masking behind a blank profile myself. Turns out I'm not alone in doing this. Oh and there is an age formula I work out too – actual age minus ten percent minus two further years. I'm letting out a sigh. Dating is cruel and complicated.

I do find a few nice men to talk too amongst the sea of darkness. There was Aaron. Physically not my type but had such energy as we talk and quickly swap to Whatsapp. He kept using voice notes though which I hated, and at times it felt more like a job interview with multiple questions about my past. This soon fizzled out. Then there was another one, and another, and another.

I would take time writing a message as I saw this as the equivalent of a first conversation and remember my mum telling me that first impressions count. Most of these carefully crafted messages get no reply at all, a good number of them just get blocked. How rude. One received a 'sit on my face and tell me how much you love me,' arrogant prick. A few, 'sorry not my type,' well at least I know where I stand, and a few resulted in proper conversations with genuine people. From this experience I did go on a few first dates, not many seconds. No thirds. A couple of guys who I chatted to formed friendships but very soon, I became one of them. In the absence of anything else meaningful, I settled for that immediate fuck like the others. Adam's online. After a while I realise why the app is called Grindr, because it does grind you down.

***

Ironically, just as I feel like I'm slowly starting to move on I wake the next day to a message from Adam. It's all a bit cryptic. He's using language which is not his everyday vocabulary. It was like we had been transported to a Jane Austin book or something.

Adam – 'Good morning, I was thinking how we met last night whilst I was in the bath. How things have moved on but still longing for what we had, what we lost. I hope you are keeping well and moving on with your life.'

Jonathan – 'Hey, keeping well yes, moving on... not really sure. Still think about you lots but starting to realise we probably need this space to work out what we want, as tough as it still feels.'

Adam – 'Still think about you too but realise now that you are not the one for me. I need someone who I can have a connection with, someone who can share their inner most thoughts and feelings. You were too closed off to do that.'

Jonathan – 'Oh okay... good to know.'

Adam – 'Well it's true, you can't connect.'

I don't reply.

Chapter 9

The night and where it went wrong

This is the hardest chapter to write. I have rewritten it three times now and continue to edit parts. Why am I struggling so much with articulating the pitfalls in our relationship and describe the night it finished? I guess it's about acceptance. Am I willing to move on? Yes, a big part of me is, but it's bloody hard. I'm also conscious of how self-indulgent it is to write in this way. I regularly tell myself off for not getting over him in a way I should and question why I continue to stop myself from moving on. Instead, I manifest in my sadness. I think it is important, however, to try and explain to you, or explain to myself, what's happened. My version anyway.

As I said before, being dumped makes you vulnerable at the best of times, being dumped whilst naked during sex brings this to a completely new dimension. It was a weekend where I was staying at Adam's and we had just come back from a beautiful long walk with Raff. Just to explain so this makes sense. About four months prior to this day, Adam finally sold his house near me and moved twenty miles to be closer to his family. Well at least that's what he said. Was it to get away from me? I'm not sure is the answer. I don't think that was the case, but I think there was a part of him that didn't want to be in our relationship, or any relationship come to that and craved independence.

Creating distance physically allowed him start to build said independence. Although ironically now, having got this independence he seems desperate to lose it with another guy. I do feel slightly used in this way as I was enough when the alternative was living with his ex, but I'm understanding now that life, no people, are more complicated than this. Also, if I'm truly honest, I was quiet, withdrawn and not present during the end of our relationship. I see that now, but I was blinded at the time. Only coming out the other side can I look back more objectively on what we had.

It was a normal day, we had lunch out in a pub followed by a trip to the garden centre for plants. Sounds very established couple like, doesn't it? We both loved plants and were each creating our very own tropical rain forests with the long-term goal of combining them, or at least that's what I thought, based largely on the fact that this is what he used to say. Nothing seemed unusual, we chatted in our normal way throughout the walk; work stuff, family stuff, the latest box set we had been watching. Come to think about it, these exchanges in conversation had started to feel a bit contrived. Granted, I am a quiet person generally. I've always followed the rule of if I can say it in five words rather than fifty, I will. I apply that to all settings in my life. Perhaps I was quieter than usual; was I? I don't actually think I was. I didn't feel any awkwardness, which I later learn Adam did.

In truth, I resented Adam moving away because it felt like a step backwards in our relationship. Even though at the time I knew I was not ready to move in with him and sell my flat, which I loved so much. The arrangement of just seeing Adam at weekends was not working for me. I still wanted to be with him, and share our lives together, so what other option did I have? Instead, I focused on the long-term goal as I was confident we could have an amazing life together. Adam said initially he needed six months. 'I'll do the flat up really quickly, make some money on it, and then we can talk about whether we buy somewhere together at that stage or what we do.' But as Adam started to enjoy his independence that six months suddenly became eighteen months to two years.

After a drink, yes a cup of tea, we decided to have a late afternoon snooze. Again, this is something we were accustomed to. I introduced him to the joys of an afternoon nap. Right, how can I summarise this whilst still composing mine and Adam's dignity? I can't really. On waking we started to make love. I say make love, Adam might correct me and say we were having sex. For a while he was feeling that the passion in our relationship had faded away, but again kept this gem to himself. Perhaps it had to some degree. I was not really in the mood for sex, but I felt I ought to, as pathetic as that sounds. I was leaving later that day and we had not had sex all weekend. I wasn't feeling too great the Friday night, then we were up early on the Saturday, I was then leaving that Saturday night – I'm not sure why I was not there the full weekend? Anyhow, there were a few times when we could have had sex but didn't so I felt we should. Just writing this now it feels too mechanical. I thought as a young (ish) couple in a relatively new (ish) relationship, that was the thing to do. The expectation, the norm.

We kissed, we fondled, we caressed. About twenty minutes in, I start to lose my erection. For some reason I was in my head. What was I thinking about? I'm not sure really. It wasn't what shall I have for tea later. It was deeper than this. Was I picking up on Adam and feeling something was not quite right for him? Was it the pressure to perform knowing that I wasn't really in the mood? Did I actually fancy him? A combination of all these things, I think. It is strange to question my admiration and affection for Adam as I did, and still do, love him which is shown by my obsession and reluctance to let go. I guess I had been in my head for a while. Fuck, I've been in my head ever since our first parting. Actually, I've been in my head ever since we first met where I questioned what he saw in me. Back to the night, Adam took over and took me from behind and no one spoke of what happened.

We carried on kissing and Adam went to ride me. Whilst just a couple of minutes in I lost my erection again. Or at least started too. Adam moved position, this time he laid face down on his knees. I don't know why but I wasn't expecting this. I thought he was going to lie on his back. This was my favourite position. I didn't say anything. Why not? I started to masturbate to get hard again. As I did Adam started to laugh. I guess it was a nervous awkward laugh, but it was enough to stop me ever getting hard again. Adam knew that he could have made me hard by playing with my nipples. I loved this as it was as if they were wired to my cock. He didn't. I could have also asked him to do this but I just stayed quiet. Instead, we allowed this embarrassment to unfold.

'What's going on? What's happening?' Adam asked.

'I don't know.'

Whilst we're both naked he tells me that he does not want to be with me anymore. That for a while it hasn't felt right. That he feels nervous around me. That he can't be himself. That I was only seventy percent of what he wanted. I later learn through a series of text messages that he also felt there was no passion. No love making and it was just sex. Well judging by that afternoon there wasn't even that. He wanted more which I think was the ultimate reason why he ended the relationship. I question why I could not give more if this was indeed the case. By that statement I accept that there was no passion. Well some passion. It did drift towards the end. Why? Did I truly love Adam? Or do you replace the word 'love' for 'care'? But if that's true, why am I struggling so much to move on and why did things at the start of our relationship feel so right? Fuck, I don't know.

Now you would think I would be used to this. We've been here before as we had split a few times in the two years we were together. This time, however, it took me totally by surprise. The promises made when we split up previously, where we said we would talk to each other if we had any issues. What happened to that? I get out of bed. I think I'm in a state of shock but I'm still questioning if this is final or not. I'm feeling confused. I put on some clothes, take my already packed bag and call Raff. I'm about to leave when Adam speaks.

'I'm going to need my key back.'

It was said with such directness. Okay this now feels final. I hand Adam his key in exchange for mine, and then I leave.

Feelings of emptiness. It's hard to articulate what I'm feeling at this point. I guess I'm in a daze. Driving home my head tries, at speed, to process the events of the last hour. I drive at speed too. I later get a speeding fine sent to me. I don't know why I'm rushing. There is nothing for me to get back for. I pull into a petrol station with a craving for a cigarette. I've not smoked in twenty years but feel the need to start a new toxic relationship.

'Ten Marlborough Lights please.'

The assistant looks confused, 'You mean Marlborough Gold, and you can't get ten anymore, only twenty.'

'Oh okay … twenty of those please, and a lighter.'

As I light the cigarette I'm greeted by a harsh taste in my mouth, I push through as I know the next one will be better. Back home I walk into an empty cold flat. I walk to my fridge and reach for the wine and as I pour, I'm reassured by the glogging sound of the wine dropping to the glass. Notes of plums and barley meet my mouth. Cheap Aldi shit but it serves a purpose. I then phone Adam. Why? Why the fuck would I do this? He doesn't answer and instead sends a text:

Adam – Home Safe?

Jonathan – Hi…Not sure why I'm ringing to be honest… didn't know if there was anything unresolved which we need to talk about although things seemed pretty final when I left. Yes, home safe.

Just like that, our relationship ended.

***

I often try and pinpoint the exact moment when our relationship was beyond return. I reflect on a scene, yes I'm referring to it as a scene, as I have replayed that moment in my head multiple times so it now feels like a film. We had just had sex one Sunday afternoon. I managed to get it up that time. I put on some clothes and put the kettle on to make a cup of tea. This became something of a ritual. Whilst waiting for the kettle I was on the balcony and was joined by Adam wearing just a jock. Walkers looked up, a couple with their dog, and couldn't miss the semi-naked man flaunting himself so confidently. Rather than feeling proud, or just not caring what others think, I thought 'put some clothes on'. I felt embarrassment for some reason. My prudishness was coming out. I didn't say anything, not consciously, but Adam heard what I was thinking and that was the start of a deeper message between us.

Before this though there were other cracks. We had broken up four times previously. Despite our break ups we kept coming back to each other, there was this magnetic pull. I think I took on a caring role, and he accepted this. I think that's why it's so hard to let go now, because I still deeply love and care for him. I want to protect him, and whilst having those qualities is important, in a healthy partnership, I don't think our quantities were quite right. On the one hand I became his carer, but I was also closed to him. That's going to fuck someone up. My god I was like this Victorian Nanny. No wonder he started to feel the way he did. No wonder he wanted out.

I realise now that we wanted different things. I sometimes question if I ever wanted him at all. Just moments before he kissed me that first night I was thinking he would make a good friend and that's where I was anticipating things were going.

I then got swept away with everything. Overtime I started to question his sincerity and intentions and whether I was enough for him. These insecurities grew to demons. I've just re read these words and I questioned his sincerity, yet from the start I was ambiguous about our relationship so how come I transferred this on to him? Was I responsible for the demise from the outset? And now I'm carrying on like a deranged person unable to let go. Head fuck. Adam, I'm sorry. It was my fault all along and I stole two years of your life.

Chapter 10

Where it really went wrong

With social media and the technology we all own, it has never been so easy to cheat in a relationship, but it's also never been so easy to get caught. I first suspected Adam when he received a Facebook messenger notification on his phone one morning. I didn't purposely look for it, but it just popped up as I was in the kitchen making food whilst Adam was sleeping. I glanced across as the lit screen caught my attention. I don't remember the exact words now but it was along the lines of, 'would be good to meet up sometime'. I stewed for a while before returning to the bedroom with two cups of tea in hand. As I placed one cup next to Adam's head I could see he was awake.

'Who's Paul?'

'Paul, I don't know.'

'Well he wants to meet up sometime.'

Adam paused for a few seconds, which felt longer.

'Paul is going out with Lewis. They are friends of mine. He's just messing around and joking. He's flirtatious in that way, it doesn't mean anything.'

Surprisingly, I very easily let any thoughts regarding infidelity go. It's a bit like now where I'll sometimes have a cigarette immediately after another one. I know I shouldn't do it, I know smoking is bad for me, but I switch my brain off to that thought. Eating cake for some would be another example. I've done this, as I'm sure others have, my whole life starting with my sexuality where I knew I didn't like girls. I would fantasise about my male teachers at school, yet still not accept I was gay.

Then a few weeks later, Adam booked cinema tickets on his phone and couldn't retrieve them, as he was going into settings to try and resolve the issue I saw the Grindr app on his phone. I didn't say anything. Instead we went to the cinema and I pretended that everything was ok. 'You're quiet, are you sure you're okay?' he asked.

'Yes just thinking of work stuff'. Really, I was dwelling on what I had seen.

Later that evening I just came out with it and told him that I saw the app. He convincingly told me that he just goes online as a way of feeling in control. He would chat anonymously to guys and at the point of arranging a meet would block them. I found this very odd at the time but accepted his explanation. Why? It was obviously bollocks. I guess I didn't want to believe the truth and preferred to live in his lie rather than my reality. That makes me really weak doesn't it? That night we went to bed, we still had sex and I just let those thoughts go. Or at least tried to.

I couldn't let them go though, that question stayed in my head and I wanted something more concrete. The next morning I was awake early, and in the kitchen whilst Adam slept. I thought if I just saw his phone for any evidence which backs his statement. My first attempt I cracked his password. It was his date of birth. Hardly the enigma. Then scrolling through I could see that he had seen other guys. He even slept with a friend of his who he had visited a few weeks ago. A numbness feels my body. I don't say anything however, I just pretend everything is okay.

My guide to telling if someone is cheating on

you:

1. Are there changes to their phone habits – are there security features added or are they doing anything differently like taking it to the toilet with them or having it on silent or placing it face down. Why would you place a phone face down as you are likely to scratch the screen so me thinks you are hiding something from me.

2. Other thing with the phone – all of a sudden deleting message history.

3. Oh another phone one. For Whatsapp, have they got the setting where it doesn't show if a message has been read? My friend Chris has a name for these people, they are called Fuckboys.

4. Are there physiological changes in the person. I remember deliberately referring to Grindr in a conversation with Adam once. I did it to see how he would react. He didn't blush which is the obvious sign, but his eyes went a bit watery as he talked. I started to learn that he did this when he was lying to me. The bastard. Their swallow is another thing, all of a sudden does it become more like a gulp?

5. Are there irregularities in certain things. I noticed Adam would normally do a 45 minute run, but every so often would do a 90 minute run. I didn't think to question this but what was that all about?

6. Are there changes in how often they want to have sex? Adam was incredibly passionate and

had a very high libido. Yet sometimes he was just not into it.

7. They start asking about your day such as what time you will be back, or what time you are leaving.

8. You spot a dating app on their phone. Yeah, bit of a giveaway really.

I start to learn when Adam is online. He always describes himself as Muscular looking for anonymous play and he can't spell the word discreet. He spells it discrete. I want to correct him but I resist. Even though I find this highly annoying. I know this should not be my focus, my focus should be his desire to be with others over me. The fact that I am not good enough.

Rather than confront him though, I accept this is the relationship we have, and I start to do the same. On the rare nights Adam is not at mine, I too am on Grindr as a blank profile, or a headless body image I screenshotted from an ASOS model, and I have sex. Sex that I don't particularly enjoy or want, but for some messed up reason I feel I should be getting it because I know he is.

I later learn from one of our many break ups that Adam knew I was online. Of course he didn't know that I knew he was cheating on me, his response was probably similar to mine in feeling inadequate. I'm not justifying either of us here, an affair is a reaction to something that is not right in the first place. There were underlying flaws in our relationship from the start, for whatever reason we were not prepared to admit them.

Weeks go by and I try and enjoy what we have. Most of the time I do but occasionally my mind drifts and I picture him with other guys. To prevent this from influencing me sexually (well this worked most of the time, not that night however) I convince myself that it's a turn on that he's recently been with another guy. I start to think, 'I wonder if another guy has been inside him directly before me?' The thought excites me. It's odd how I begin to think in this way. I guess the alternative is what? Hurt, disgust, anger? Although deep down, that's probably how I'm really feeling.

One time during a break, we talked about the infidelity and whether an open relationship would be more suited to us. I didn't want this, I still dreamed of the perfect relationship where we share everything (but STIs) and having someone who I trust completely. Adam said that this was what he wanted too. In reality I don't think he knew what he wanted.

At the risk of stereotyping, there appears to be a higher proportion of gay men who have an open relationship. I've been reflecting on this and I think some men are able to look at the act of sex in a mechanical way. That it's nothing more than physical satisfaction. We didn't have this though as there was emotion involved, there was deceit. This led me to stay in my head a lot. I didn't like the person I was when I was with Adam. How did I become that person who would check someone's phone when they had left the room or took a bath, yet found it completely acceptable to cheat on him too? Why did I stay? And an even bigger question, why am I struggling to move on? I do, however, start to move on. Well, I start having sex again.

Chapter 11

Monday

Name: Lee
Height: 6'4
Weight: 187lb
Ethnicity: White
Relationship Status: Open Relationship

Lee – Hi
Lee sends a photo of his face.
Jonathan – Hey there … Nice pic! What are you looking for on here?

Lee – Thanks. Mostly fun as I'm partnered. You?

Jonathan – Fun is good. I'm recently single so not looking for anything heavy. What are you into sexually?

Lee – I'm pretty open minded. Vers but more top usually. You?

Jonathan – I'm Versatile Bottom. Where do you live? Travel or accommodate?

Lee – Cool. Happy to travel if you are fairly near to the train station. Generally free some afternoons and weekends.

Jonathan – I live 5 minutes walk from the train station. Pretty flexible with times/days.

Lee – Cool got any more pics?

I send a torso pick.

Jonathan – You got body pic?

Lee sends three photographs. Two of torso and one of him wearing white boxer shorts.

Jonathan – And what are you into? Kissing, sucking, wanking, fucking and nipple play works for me.

Lee – Yeah love all of that. Love a guy to ride me. Poppers fun too.

Jonathan – You play safe?

Lee – Always play safe.

Jonathan – Good, me too.

Lee – Good man. Any nudes?

Jonathan – Not on here.

Lee – Ok. You free this afternoon?

Jonathan – Yes. Apart from walking my dog at some point I have no plans.

Lee – Touch base in a bit then.

Jonathan – Ok.

Lee – Hi again. Still up for meeting?

Jonathan – Yes what time you thinking?

Lee – There is a 4.30 train. I'll let you know when I set off.

Jonathan – Great. You should get here for 4.45 then. Address is 10 Tree view Apartments.

Lee – Ok. Would have to get the 6pm back though.

Jonathan – Gives us an hour?

Lee – Ok.

Lee – Getting on the train now.

Jonathan – Great, see you in a bit.

Lee – Here.

As I open the door I'm first struck by how tall he is. His profile did say 6'4 but seeing it in writing and seeing the person in front of you are two separate things. Raff is all excited. For so long it has just been him and me, so any attention is gratefully accepted. 'You found it okay?'

'Yes no trouble at all.'

'Oh good, can I get you a drink of anything?' This is the polite thing to ask, and the polite response is accepting a glass of water. Lee, however, is unaware of this rule.

'Yes, what do you have?'

'Water... or alcohol wise I have beer, red wine, a G&T, or soft drinks I have squash, tea, coffee, hot chocolate?'

'I'll have a hot chocolate.'

Really, I think to myself, I added that option as a joke. Who has hot chocolate before they are about to hook up? I should have offered him Bovril to see if he would have accepted that. 'Cream and sprinkles?' I ask, again jokingly.

'No thanks,' he replies.

As I'm preparing his hot chocolate we make awkward small talk. He only has a few sips before we venture into the bedroom.

In the bedroom we start to kiss. I have to stand on tip toes, but the embrace feels good if not a bit chocolatey. I start thinking that he kisses differently to Adam. Stronger, firmer, but still enjoyable. We continue to kiss, now more passionately and our bodies collide. I like the closeness. I miss that. He takes his top off and starts removing mine. We kiss again, this time our bare chests rubbing against each other. He initiates us to the bed. I'm impressed by my flexibility as I manage to slowly lower my body to the bed whilst still kissing, leaving him hovering over me on the bed. Thank you yoga.

We continue to caress each other's body. He quickly learns that I like my nipples played with. 'You like that,' he says. I think that he plays with them more softly than what Adam would. I notice that I'm in my head. That's ironic. This time comparing him to Adam. He's a good looking guy, not gym fit like Adam but he is in good shape. I enjoy being next to him and being close to someone. Our jeans come off and I pull down his Pierre Cardin pants. He's hard. I start sucking him. He moves to my nipples again and with his lips against my right nipple, I look down at his right ear and notice it is the same shape and size as Adam's ear. I imagine for a moment I am with Adam and the feelings intensify. He then moves to sucking me and I hold his head firm in the same way I did Adam's. I think his shoulders are quite alike too and I continue to imagine Adam and I making love.

By now Raff starts barking from the other room. A lot. He is not used to visitors and Adam and I would always have the door open. Often Raff would be at the foot of the bed sleeping whilst we made mad passionate love. There was one time when his little head was bopping up and down so much from our activity, he looked like one of those mini statue things you see in backs of cars. Oh and another time we woke him up and the stare he gave us was absolutely priceless, his eyes cut through us and angrily announced, 'will you just stop that I'm trying to sleep,' but back to Lee.

We continue, our bodies intertwined, every so often exchanging positions so one can be on top of the other. The pleasure deepened by the poppers until Lee reaches for the packet of condoms as he lays on his back ready for me to ride him. It feels good but it does feel different. I am comparing him to Adam. At one point Lee holds my hand which I think is sweet and we look into each other's eyes whilst he's inside me. A few minutes later he makes a face as if something is wrong.

'You ok?'

'Yes, try not to move.'

'Oh, I've just cum.'

As we detangled our bodies, I think Lee doesn't need to worry about whether the 6pm train will be late enough.

Small talk after sex is not the easiest thing to do as we wait for 6pm to come. Thankfully Raff is able to bridge any awkward silences. We briefly chat about where I live and where he lives whilst Lee finishes his hot chocolate, which is still warm. Lee then asks if he can use the loo. He is in there six minutes. That's quite a long time. When he comes out he says, 'Sorry tried to go, but couldn't.'

I reply, 'Oh I get that too.'

Then he leaves.

***

It did feel good being close to someone again. Even if it was short lived. I tell you what I really like though, aside from starting to rhyme like a Spice Girl's song, the thrill of not knowing who the guy is. I find it quite a turn on that within moments of meeting him at the door his tonge is down my throat and his penis is up my ass. I know that's wrong of me to say. Get used to it though as this book is a complete overshare! There's something quite freeing about that. That I can be responsible Jonathan by day who manages a team of professionals and wears a shirt and tie to work, and by night this dirty fuck boy who pleases all of the men. Well tries to anyway.

Chapter 12

Tuesday

I'm conscious of the comparisons I made to Adam last night. It's a bit creepy really. I decide to try something different.

Name: Dave
Age: 49
Weight: 181lb
Body: Average
Position: Versatile
Tribe: Discreet

Dave – Hi there, nice profile pic. Into?

Jonathan – Not sure to be honest. Looking for new experiences I guess. Recently single. Feel I need to move on but not ready for a long-term relationship.

Dave – I'm just looking for no strings fun. Usual stuff plus a few kinks.

Jonathan – Oh, kinks sounds interesting. Like what?

Dave – You ever tried water sports?

I think he's not talking canoeing or boating here.

Jonathan – No never tried it. Thought about it. Is that all your looking for, or are you into kissing etc too?

Dave – Kissing, WS, mutual wank.

I think about it for a while and, perhaps foolishly think I should try new things.

Jonathan – I could be up for that.

Dave – You free now.

Jonathan – In about an hour I can be.

Dave – You accommodate?

Jonathan – Yes.

Dave – Address?

Jonathan – 10 Tree view Apartments

Dave – Great will let you know when setting off.

Jonathan – Ok.

Dave – Getting ready to leave.

Dave – Here.

I open the door to an older man than I was expecting. Was Dave really forty-nine? At this point in my single life I had not learnt the age formula. Now I should have said, 'Oh I'm really sorry but you are not quite what I was expecting based on your photographs which I think are about ten years old.' Instead, I just let Dave in to penetrate me as that's the polite thing to do.

'I've had about two pints of water so there should be a good flow for you,' Dave said in a broad northern accent.

'Oh good,' I reply, whereas I was really thinking what the fuck am I doing? We move into the bedroom where there is an ensuite.

'If you start by getting me hard a bit, then you jump in the shower, and I'll give you my spray.' I oblige as Dave unfastens his zip to expose his large penis. I take hold and start to move my hand up and down as Dave starts to get erect. I question in my head whether this was the best approach as in my experience it can be harder to pee with a hard on. I carry on stroking his penis though as I decide I'm not the expert in this, but Dave is.

'Are you ready for this?' he asks.

'Yes, I am,' I respond but I'm thinking I'm really not.

'Go on strip naked and then kneel in the

shower looking up at me.'

I move to the shower slightly excited that I'm trying something new, but also thinking that maybe this something new experience could have been achieved by trying one of the specials at the local Indian takeaway. I'm in this now. I have a naked man in my bedroom with a big penis and full bladder though so there is no going back.

Kneeling in a small cubicle is not the most comfortable of positions and I regret doing legs at the gym the previous day. I don't know whether to stare at Dave or stare at his penis. I decide to stare at the latter and at this point realise how ugly penises are. What is the fascination with them? I wait for what feels a long time.

'Ok it's starting to come now.'

I do this nodding and uuhh thing at this stage. A small dribble is released, he's not at full flow and as a result it misses me but goes down the gap between the tiles and the shower tray. I desperately try not to shout at him as I fear that will not help with his flow.

'It's coming, more is coming,' he says, but it's not, it's still just dribbling on my floor. That's going to take me ages to clean that up, I think. Then finally it is released, he sprays it over my chest and over my face. I feel the heat of his urine as it gushes over my body. Two pints is quite a lot, and it continues to flow until it returns to a small dribble again, and yes goes in between the gap of the shower tray and the tiles. He shakes his penis and then leaves to get dressed as I have a shower. What just happened, I think. I reach an all-time low.

When Dave leaves Raff is fascinated by the ensuite, a room he has never ventured into before. Even he looks up at me shamefully. It takes four showers before I feel clean again and a whole litre of disinfectant before my bathroom floor is returned to the state it was previously in. I question how that is a thing, as I took no pleasure from it. That night I treat myself to that special from the takeaway and agree, in a pact with Raff, never to speak about Dave ever again.

Chapter 13

Wednesday

Name: Baz
Age: 52
Weight: 76kg
Height: 175cm
Body: Toned
Ethnicity: White
Position: Versatile
Relationship Status: Single

Jonathan – Hey there, you ok?

Baz – Yeah, I'm ok. You ok?

Jonathan – I like your profile. You visiting or live here?

Baz – I like yours too. I'm visiting.

Jonathan – Cool. Looking for fun whilst here?

Baz – I see you live here.

Baz – I am.

Jonathan – Travel or accommodate?

Baz – Give me 10 mins please, I have something to do.

Jonathan – Sure.

10 minutes later.

Baz – Could do either. How about you?

Jonathan – Just logged off computer from work and feeling horny. You looking for now or later?

Baz – I'm just packing up at work any time after an hour.

Jonathan – Could work.

Jonathan – And what are you up for doing?

Baz – I love playing, wild to mild.

Jonathan – Wild sounds good.

Baz – Great answer.

Baz – And love a long chilled session.

Jonathan – Sounds good.

Baz – Staying in a hotel here.

Jonathan – Cool, I could come to you if you like?

Baz – Ok great. I'm staying in the Premier Inn in town.

Jonathan – Yeah I know it. What time?

Baz – Need to check in first. An hour or so.

Jonathan – I might do a quick gym session first then. Make it 90 minutes.

Baz – Perfect.

Jonathan – Still on?

Baz – Yeah def.

Jonathan – Leaving now, 15 minutes.

Baz – Okay great.

Jonathan – Here.

Baz – Okay, give me 5 minutes, I'll come down to you.

As I'm driving to see Baz I'm not sure how well this meeting will go. What's Baz short for anyway, I think? He looks a bit like a hillbilly from his profile pictures with a shaved head and really long beard, but I'm convinced there is a good body under those dungarees so I'm willing to give it a go. Hey, I've started to whore it up so I might as well continue. I find the hotel and as I park up, I text him to let him know that I've arrived.

Jonathan – Here.

Baz – Okay, give me 5 minutes, I'll come down to you.

I waited anxiously outside as I saw this very hip and trendy man walk through the sliding doors of the hotel. He's shorter than I thought but much more attractive. I can feel myself getting excited.

'You smoke?'

'As in normal cigarettes? I have the odd one.' That's a lie, I've been smoking like an absolute trooper.

'You want one?' He offers me a cigerallo. I haven't seen one of those for years, my English teacher, Mrs Wagstaff used to smoke them. Back then it was acceptable for her to smoke in her office which adjoined the classroom.

'They are like a small cigar with a filter,' Baz informs me.

'Sure.'

As we smoke, we speak slightly clumsily about our work. He works in TV production and travels a lot. I start to think he's a sweet guy. We also chat about the weather, like you do, and the city which is a new place for him.

'Wanna come up then?' I follow him up to his room where I kiss him on the lips, but he does not respond with a great deal of passion.

'Make yourself comfortable,' he says as he takes my coat to hang it up.

'I'm just going to have a quick bath as I did not think there was time before,' he informs me. I think there's no time now as I'm already here. I assume by bath he must mean shower, but was then surprised to see him in the mirror lying in a pool of bubbles. Okay this is a bit odd. He shouts a few questions as I lie in his hotel bed not really sure what to do. I join him in the bathroom.

'Take a seat,' he gestures to the toilet. We talk about his flat in London. I can't remember how we got onto that conversation now but as we do, he keeps topping up his bath with more hot water. Does he actually want to have sex I think to myself? Fifteen minutes in I'm about to ask if he wants me to go or stay and then I notice his hard on. This is promising I think to myself.

'Do you want a towel?' I'm starting to get impatient now, so I think I'll be bolder.

'Yes, that would be great.' I pass him the towel, but slowly, as he emerges from the water, his skin all glossy and smooth looking. I was right to think he had a good body. I think it was just nervousness. As we move to the bedroom, he loses those nerves.

We kiss, this time much more passionately as we kneel on the bed facing each. He gets two pillows and places one under my thighs and one under his to stop our legs from aching. I assume this is why anyway. This is someone with experience. We continue to kiss and caress each other's body. He stands up in front of me, his penis rock hard as I place it to my mouth. It looked very veiny I think to myself. This lasts five minutes as he tells me to suck harder, which I don't question and continue to do. As he removes it from my mouth he lies down on the bed where we continue to kiss and touch each other's body.

'You have amazing tattoos,' he compliments me. All of a sudden, he announces that he has to ring Julie. Who the fuck is Julie? I think to myself.

'Julie, is my work colleague, I need to know if

she has booked a hotel for tomorrow.' Okay, let's bring Julie into this, I think. He rings Julie but she does not pick up.

'I'm just going to book a hotel room myself,' he says as he searches for hotels.

We are still completely naked, he's on all fours with his back to me as he's scrolling through hotels. I now think, right well what do I do now? He then says to me, 'you can rim me if you like?' This isn't really my thing but in the absence of anything else to do I start to rim him. I find myself getting quite turned on by this.

'Can I fuck you?' I ask.

'Sure.'

As I enter him he feels amazing, he's not showing any interest in what I'm doing other than giving the odd grunt as I push myself deeper into him. Whilst I'm fucking him, sorry I'm trying to find a better word but that's what it was, his head is bobbing whilst still tapping away. We stop as I read him the CVI number on the back of his credit card. He's finally booked his hotel, so we return, this time to a different position of him on his back.

'Let your hair down,' he asks. My hair is getting long and I have it tied back. I release my hair and as I do I shake it free as if I'm in a hair commercial. We continue to have sex.

'I was not expecting that, where did that come from?'

'I know,' I reply with equal surprise.

It's now been two hours where we've taken it in turns fooling around with each other. I explain that I need to leave to get back to my dog.

'It's been a really good evening.'

'It has, hasn't it?'

I leave feeling good about myself and good about dating. Well, not dating, these are hook ups. I feel good about the future.

Back home I log into Grindr. It's now habitual. There is a message from Baz.

Baz – Really enjoyable evening. It was lovely meeting you Jonathan.

I reply.

Jonathan – Yes you too. Was going to message you. A) What is the name of those cigarette things? B) Would you like to keep in touch? Here is my number.

Baz – Yes definitely. I travel a lot but hope to be back here soon. And they are called Cigerallos.

He sends a photo of him holding them.

Jonathan – Oh that's good. Right, going to bed now. Night

Baz – Night Tarzan.

***

It's time for another Dear Diary moment… I'm actually frickin proud of myself tonight. I had fun with Baz. I felt confident. That new experience with Baz where I topped him despite those fears and insecurities of what happened last time I did this, you know. I didn't think about it I just did it, and I became Tarzan. Go me!

Chapter 14

Thursday

Name: Ryan
Age: 35
Height: 5'9
Body Type: Muscular
Position: Top
Tribes: Clean-Cut
Relationship Status: Single
Meet At: Your Place

I set about finding another meet. I'm not sure why exactly, this seems to be my life right now. I was not going to meet anyone tonight but find myself scrolling through the profiles again late at night and like a moth to a flame I'm drawn to the array of torsos, head shots and blank boxes in front of me. Ryan stands out as a fit attractive guy just four miles away from me. We start to chat.

Ryan – Good evening. You're up late.

Jonathan – Yes I can't sleep. Tried but gave up so here I am.

Ryan – Ha, the same. I'm in bed but can't sleep.

Ryan – Not seen you on here before.

Jonathan – Yes, newish profile. Recently, ish, single.

Ryan – I'm sorry to hear that man. You ok?

Jonathan – Yes getting there.

Ryan – Relationships can be tough. How long you been single for? What happened, if you don't mind me asking?

Jonathan – Just over 3 months now. Complicated relationship, too much to explain in a text tbh. I guess we just worked out that we were not right for each other.

Ryan – Stay positive, you never know what is around the corner.

Jonathan – Thanks. You seem nice. A rarity on here!

Ryan – Tell me about it, so many time wasters and pic collectors.

Jonathan – Been so tempted to delete this app so many times.

Ryan – I'm glad you didn't.

Jonathan – Really. Why?

Ryan – Cos you look hot from your photos.

Jonathan – Awww thanks. Looking good there too.

Ryan – What do you do for a living?

Jonathan – Very boring, work in marketing. You?

Ryan – Retail Manager.

Jonathan – Long hours.

Ryan – Yes, should really be sleeping as early start tomorrow but...

As Ryan arrives at my flat we waste no time in making our way to the bedroom. As we kiss, we both get hard, and Ryan grabs my crouch and starts squeezing it. My hands work their way up Ryan's T-Shirt as I massage his firm flat torso. He takes his shirt off to reveal a masculine physique which I start to kiss. Our lips met again and we continue. He's a good kisser, I think. I'm making less comparisons to Adam and I'm able to enjoy the moment. Jeans, top, socks, pants all came off and scattered the floor. They're entangled as if the clothes are a metaphor for what is about to happen.

Trapped in eye contact we stare intently, both bare, both facing each other as if we are in battle or stags locking horns. Our chests pump and our hearts beat profusely in excitement.

Simultaneously we step closer as if we are in dance, now our chests rub up against each other.

We fall onto the bed and continue to kiss. There is a raw passion to the encounter as we both hold each other firmly. With Ryan pinned to the bed, I make my way down, kiss by kiss, to his throbbing penis which I feel at the back of my throat. Ryan, not content on just being sucked, thrusts his penis more causing me to gag. He makes no apologies and then reciprocates the act on me. His hands reach for the condoms which I previously arranged on the bedside table when I knew Ryan was going to be coming and, as the ordered person I am, lined up in size order; lube, poppers, condoms.

On my knees, Ryan enters me with force. I let out a pleasurable sigh as he continues to thrust. His body is sweaty. I start to taste it and cannot stop licking the salty sweat from his arms. Ryan releases his cock from my body, but not for long as he then swings me around onto my back where he continues. We lock horns again and Ryan drops out of character and gives a big smile as he sees my enjoyment. As he does, I play with my cock.

'I'm getting close,' whispers Ryan.

'Me too.'

We both cum at the same time, I shoot a massive load which reaches Ryan's shoulder. We both start to laugh as we collapse in each other's arm.

'Wow, I really needed that,' Ryan shares.

'Yes, I did too.'

We lie there in silence for a short time before he gets up and starts getting dressed.

'Do you want a shower?'

'No it's okay it's getting pretty late, I better dash.'

Ryan quickly gets dressed and within moments I'm on my own again. I can smell him on my skin and on the pillow which I like. I decline to shower too as I want to preserve what we have for longer. A strange comfort that takes me to sleep.

Chapter 15

Friday

Name: Kink
Age: 46
Height: 5'11
Ethnicity: White
Body Type: Average
Gender: Man
Position: Versatile
Tribes: Leather
Relationship Status: Single
Looking For: Chat, Networking, Right Now

Kink, or Gene to give him his real name which I find out after a few text exchanges, approaches me with a question.

Kink – Would you let me keep your pants after we have sex?

Jonathan – I'm sorry, what?

Kink – It's my thing. I like to keep a man's pants after having sex.

Jonathan – Sure.

I think to myself, if this does happen, I'm not going to be wearing my best boxers. Oh, but I can't wear my really old ones either, dilemma.

Kink – I like to have loads of pants laid out on the bed, and then I'll ask you to model them for me. And I'll choose which ones I take home.

Okay, I think. Do I have enough pants to potentially part with one of them.

Jonathan – Are you into other stuff too? Or just pants?

Kink – I like mutual oral and wanking too.

Jonathan – Okay I could be up for that.

Kink – Are you free later?

Jonathan – Yes I'm free all evening.

Kink – You able to accommodate?

Jonathan – Yes I live alone.

Kink – 8pm?

Jonathan – Yes that's cool.

Kink – Have at least five or six pairs for me.

Jonathan – Okay.

Kink – Pants or Boxers?

Jonathan – I mostly wear boxers.

Kink – Perfect.

I immediately go straight to my underwear drawer to sift through what ones I would be willing to part with, I'm not just picking one now, but it will be a roulette to which pair is chosen. I would normally be choosing my best pair to wear before a date or meet, this time I'm choosing the worse. I start to think, how long can I keep this shit up? I choose five that I think would be appropriate and start to display them on my bed. Do I go for a scatter approach, or shall I put them in a particular order? I could colour code them? Or sort by preference? I initially go for the scatter effect then decide that's too untidy so just stack them in a neat pile. My phone pings.

Kink – I'm outside.

Jonathan – Okay, it's number 10.

Gene enters the flat and is more attractive than his photos, he really does not look the type to have a pant fetish, but I guess everyone has some mystery to them and no one knows what truly goes on in other people's head.

'Well, well, what do we have here?'

I start to talk about the pants as if I'm trying to sell them on a market stall. 'These have hardly been worn, they are quite tight, good elastic around the waist. Oh and these are good ones too,

115

there from Marks and Spencer's you know?'

'These look like they have been worn a lot, put these on.'

I think, do I leave the room or do I do it in front of him. 'Shall I do it here, or shall I put them on and come back?' I ask. What the fuck am I doing? I'm asking permission in my own house.

'Put them on now.'

I unbutton my jeans and take them off. I try to do this as elegantly as I can as I'm being eagerly watched. The problem is they are slim fit jeans and there is no elegant way of doing this. I stumble and grab Gene's arm to balance. I take off my original pants and put on the pair chosen by Gene. Gene picks up the worn pair and raises it to his nose to sniff. With his other hand Gene starts touching himself, I can see he is deeply aroused by what is going on.

The issue for me is that I'm not really turned on by this. I do feel slightly excited in that what I'm doing feels naughty and arousing to someone else. I stand there whilst Gene plays with himself with one hand and cups my penis with the other. This does get me more aroused. 'That's good, now start playing with yourself too.'

I oblige and start masturbating in front of him.

'Swap for these now,' he says as he hands me another pair.

'When you are ready, I want you to cum in them.'

I masturbate more vigorously, locked in eye

contact with him as I do. I can feel myself getting close.

'I'm getting close.'

'That's it, just let it out.'

As I do a wet stain starts to appear.

'Right I want you to take them off and now give them to me.'

I do, but I now feel exposed rather than excited as I stand there naked from the waist down but for socks. Gene sniffs the cum soaked boxers until he lets out an explosion in his pants too. 'Hey thanks for that, that was hot. I'm going to keep these okay?'

'Yes that's okay,' I reply.

'Can I use your bathroom?'

'Oh yes just in there,' I say directing him to the ensuite, which thankfully is now smelling normal. As he goes into the bathroom, I go to get some tracksuit bottoms from another room and meet him in the hallway where we exchange goodbyes. Gene promptly leaves. I then return to the bedroom to find Gene has taken every single pair of my pants. I let out a smile and giggle.

***

I'm now in bed with a hot chocolate. I've been craving one ever since Lee had his Monday night. I think is this what my life has become, a long line of disastrous hook ups and dates. I don't want a boyfriend, I know I need to have a period of time on my own, but equally I don't want this. I think about Adam, and then I go back to thinking about my single lifestyle. This is feeling very unfulfilling. I'm forty now and pretty sure this is not what my life should be looking like. I hate myself right now.

C h a p t e r   1 6

Saturday

Name: Dom
Age: 48
Height: 5'6
Ethnicity: White
Body Type: Toned
Position: Top
Relationship Status: Married
Looking For: Chat, Dates, Right Now

I had been talking to Stuart, profile name Dom, for a few days. It is appealing to give complete control over to somebody else and do exactly what they want. Maybe this is because I am conflicted with my own future? I know I have to move on, that deep down I am not ready for another long-term relationship but I am lonely and feeling sexually unfulfilled. Perhaps it's because I thought, or knew, Adam was acting in the same way? Or suddenly, to my surprise, I am in a place in my life again where I can do what I want. I have no responsibilities, no children to look after, I'm financially sound, well apart from the huge car payments. This is a time when I should be enjoying myself, hence this sexual freedom I'm expressing. We arrange to meet Saturday night, where I am going to go to Stuart's house.

I approach the road and turn right to where my sat nav directs me. 'Your destination can be found on the left.' I'm told. I see a space to park. As I do I see a guy outside on his phone. That's him, I think. I park, turn off the ignition and get out.

'You here for me?' the man asks.

'Yes,' I reply.

'I've been waiting a while,' the guy says quite arrogantly.

'Oh sorry', I think, I did tell him I would be twenty minutes and it's only been about fifteen.

'Okay well you are here now, I'm going to the train station.'

'You what?'

'Train station, you're my Uber right?'

'Oh no, I'm not an Uber.'

There is an awkward silence and neither of us knows what to say. I walk off and approach the house.

Stuart is a well-educated guy with a successful job in banking. He is a Master Dom who was looking for someone to be one of his subs. I had established this from our previous message exchange, along with the fact that Stuart has a husband, and they sometimes play together or apart, 'it all dependent on how I feel,' he went on to explain. Marc was his husband's name, and he was one of Stuart's subs too. He boastfully informed me that he has four subs in total, but he was looking for more and thought I had potential providing I can obey his every word.

'Do you think you can do that Jonathan, you'll be my little sub?' He says little, but at five foot six and tender physique it was Stuart who seemed little compared to me.

'Yes I can do that.'

'Yes, SIR, is what you mean.'

'Yes, Sir. Sorry.'

'That's okay, you'll get used to addressing me correctly and if you don't then I will punish you.' I wasn't sure but went along with this, boosting Stuart's ego.

I made sure to arrive promptly. I'm a prompt person anyway and hate being late for any event but on this occasion took extra care to ensure I was on time by giving myself ten-minute contingency time before setting off. As I knocked at the door, I was greeted by Stuart who let me in and told me to go into the dining room. I could hear the TV on in the other room and the sound of a dog bark.

'Just ignore them, they'll settle down in a minute, they know I have a visitor.' I make my way to the room which he directed and then I'm told to strip.

'Take them all off, I want to see you. You can leave them there on the floor. You'll get them back when I have finished.'

I oblige. I stand naked in this man's dining room, slightly conscious as the curtains are not drawn and I'm worried someone could walk past and see me, literally all of me. Stuart walks behind me and starts to circle me in a similar way to how Raff greets a dog he likes at the park. I have to say I'm slightly unnerved by this but at the same time excited. My eyes turn to the objects around the room and I notice the family photos of Stuart and Marc on the wall with others whom I assume are their extended family. They look so normal, does that sweet old lady next to him in that picture know he has four subs and a desire for more?

'Right, I want you to follow me upstairs.'

I follow.

Upstairs Stuart quizzes me on whether I have been a sub for anyone before.

'No,' I reply.

'But you like the idea of it, right?'

'Yes, I do,' but I actually think, hmmm…I'm not entirely sure. Why do I get myself in these situations?

'I want you to wear this for me.'

He gives me a chastity cage for my penis. There is a locking mechanism which he helps with. 'Now if we make this a permanent arrangement I'll get you to wear this the whole time, and I'll keep the key.'

How terribly unhygienic I think, but I reply, 'yes, I'll be up for that.'

'Now I'm going to put this on you now.' He starts putting a thick chain around my neck. I now think I must look like Mr T with it on. I try not to snigger. I wonder if Mr T has a chastity cage as well as a matching accessory? The chain is cold and heavy, and I don't like it.

We kiss. I immediately pick up on Stuart's bad breath. I'm not enjoying this. We kiss again. I can't really walk out with this chain around my neck though. Is this why he put it on me? I can't think what other purpose it serves other than humiliation which I guess fits with the whole dom/sub thing.

'I want you to start sucking me now.' I comply

and can feel Stuart's penis getting harder. I carry on in fear of being kissed again. I do this for so long my jaw starts to ache, but I think if I can get him to cum quickly, I can be released and then will have time for a Netflix episode back at home. My neck aches too from the chain. Stuart has other ideas and reaches for some lube and starts fingering me as I knee on the bed, one eye on the alarm clock.

'I've probably only got 5 or 10 minutes before I need to leave.'

Stuart seems slightly offended by this but continues before ordering me to suck him again. I continue until Stuart starts to cum. It's salty and I wonder if Stuart has been getting a balanced diet. Eat more pineapple. Before Stuart orders me to swallow I just spit it out spontaneously onto his chest.

'Sorry,' I say.

'That's ok,' he says as he reaches for a tissue and then the keys to unchain me. 'Overtime you'll learn,' he informs me. I know I won't be though.

I am unchained and as this happens I start to feel like I have my freedom back. I vow to myself not to do this again. I make little eye contact with Stuart and quietly go downstairs to where my clothes are located. I'm reminded of the fact that Marc has been watching TV with the dogs all this time. That's a tad weird, I think. I spot a plant in the hallway and think that would look good in my apartment as I dress. Stuart tells me that he had a good time and for us to keep in touch.

'Oh I will,' I reply. Driving back I think how stupid I have been. All this week. Anything could have happened to me. When I get back home I'm greeted by Raff who is as pleased to see me as ever. I pick him up and give him a big cuddle. The shame, I think. Never again. I reach for my phone.

'Dear Stuart, thank you for earlier. I had a really good time. I don't quite think I'm Sub material though as much fun as it was. But thank you.' What else could I do? I could hardly tell a Master Dom that his breath stinks!

Chapter 17

Sunday

By the time Sunday comes I realise I've spent copious amounts of time on this app. It's started to become an obsession. My phone informs me that my weekly screen time is up by 59% for an average of 5 hours and 26 minutes a day. This is because of Grindr. It's the first thing I check in the morning, and then last thing at night. Between these hours I am glued to seeing who's online? Who's near? Who's viewed? It is now 2pm and apart from walking Raff I have nothing to show for my day as

I have just spent it scrolling through profiles. A message pops up.

Name: Top
Age: 42
Height: 6'2
White: 179lbs
Ethnicity: White
Body Type: Average
Position: Top
Tribes: Otter
HIV Status: Negative

Top – Hey there. You looking for fun?

I think for a second and realise that I'm not. The profile of 'Top' is encouraging, but I take myself to the bathroom, I have a wank, and then do something productive with the rest of the day. I go to the gym and come back feeling good about myself. I realise this is the way forward. The number of hours spent on that app which are just lost. I just feel horrible about myself afterwards. Don't get me wrong, there was excitement talking to the guys I met, pleasure in the activity itself, well mostly pleasure, I have to tell you there were some guys who didn't make the cut. One guy greeted me in a cow boy hat, another who was so much older than his photos I told him so and asked him to leave (he then accused me of being on drugs) and another guy turned up saying he couldn't be long as he had his grandad waiting in the car outside! Even the good ones, I would still be left feeling low. I decide that things have to change. I've had a week of whoring it up, but that's not who I am, or who I want to be.

Why am sharing such graphic detail about my sex life? Do you really want to know? What purpose does it serve? I'm very conscious as I write about my sexual encounters, I'm portraying the gay dating scene in a poor light. There is a responsibility I hold, and I don't know whether I am doing this a disservice. Not everyone sleeps around, but is this bad anyway? I'm single again at forty, which I was not anticipating. There is a risk that I am putting myself in by just turning up at random blokes houses where no one knows where I am. I do sometimes think what would happen to Raff if anything happened to me. When I leave, I top his bowl of water to the maximum, but this would only extend his life for maybe an extra day? He could just become trapped in the flat and just die alone from thirst or starvation. He doesn't bark so would he alert anyone? I always leave my front door unlocked for this reason.

Other than my risk taking though, what harm am I causing? I didn't take psychology but is this where its argued women are less likely to take similar risks as there is something about the desire for reproduction? I'm not bothered by that. I call it the ripple effect. Some people, breeders, which in the gay world means something else entirely but I use this term meaning people who have children, have kids because they want to leave a legacy. Not everyone does, and I know I'm vastly generalising. I've seen friends do it where they give up on their lives and live vicariously through their children. I have no desire to do this. Is this what my promiscuity is? Experiencing as much pleasure as I can because I know that when I'm dead, there will be no more and I have no one, other than Raff, reliant on me?

So, if I'm not hurting anyone, is it okay for me to behave like a slut? I've just googled the meaning of a slut and according to the Cambridge Dictionary, it is 'a woman who has sexual relationships with a lot of men without any emotional involvement.' I find it fascinating that the definition is referring to just women. So, what is the terminology for a male slut? Siri tells me it is a 'gigolo' but goes on to say, 'it may not be quite as low-class or dirty as "slut", it's probably close enough to meet most needs.' Thanks for that Siri. Just going back to the slut definition, it's the term itself which has the connotations of being bad. Why is this? How many men have sexual relationships without emotional involvement? This seems acceptable, but not for women? I'll move away from this gender inequality in a minute as I'm probably not doing it justice as I'm one of the least political people you could meet, but this terminology does seem wrong.

I'm reflecting on things further and repeating the words 'emotional involvement' and I think that is what I'm struggling with. I was burnt by Adam with showing any emotional attachment. Despite how he perceives it, I was emotionally invested in our relationship and now am I frightened about showing this explosure again. Just how will I be when it comes to finding a long-term partner? Will I be able to give my all, or will I be holding back? Much like how Adam felt I was holding back. In many ways I guess I was.

I know I'm digressing again. I was questioning the appropriateness of the graphic detail I have been recording in here, which led me to reflect on my own behaviour from a sense of morality, but I skimmed the part about why am I sharing so much? There is part of me that thinks, why not? Writing about gay sex is liberating for me and I feel it is important that this is discussed as much as heterosexual sex. I'm not the type of person who would talk about sex in person, am I hiding behind these words? Not sure. There is also something quite comical about having my pants stolen or Dave pissing on my floor which I hope you find amusing too. I do hope I'm not offending anyone. Although if I was, I think you would have stopped reading by now.

***

Adam's emailed me. No, it's not 1992. It's just he blocked me from Whatsapp and mobile phone from our last exchange. At first I thought email was a better form of communication for us, rather than replying instantly, there is a time delay so you can think about what you are saying before sending. We still manage to upset each other. He's asking how I'm doing and saying that he still misses me. I feel the same but I also think nothing's changed. My responses are, what I think, well thought out, polite but not misleading. Somehow he thinks I'm being rude. I'm now getting the drama of a relationship, without the make-up sex. Great.

Chapter 18

Dates

Right, a new rule. No casual meets and no hook ups. It might fulfil part of me, but I'm left feeling empty afterwards. I'm only going to go on proper dates, and I am not going to kiss a guy until at least a second date. Let us return to how things were before Grindr and other dating apps. Although was this really how things were before social media? I'm not sure, I never experienced the gay night club scene or any dating scene. Through university I was not out and then met Tom when I was twenty and we were together for fifteen years. Either way, I have a new rule and I'm sticking to it.

As a result of this rule, my social life becomes the Sahara desert. I've still got most of those condoms I was given from the Sexual Health Clinic. Are there expiry dates on them? I go on a few dates and find that I like talking to people and hearing their stories. I've always been fascinated by people. In the past I have bought books on body language and Fliss, a friend of mine, and I would often people watch and give elaborate back stories about the people we see. 'I bet they are on a first date,' 'it's his birthday and he is with his brother and that's their partners' or 'he's recently widowed and has ventured out of the house for the first time.' We would do this for hours. Once we were overheard naming a person's child and they looked at us somewhat alarmingly. I know that I am a people person and overtime I learn that I can communicate with people too. Not in a sexual way which recently has been how I met most people in my life, but through mutual conversation. I enjoy listening to find out about the events that have brought someone to that exact spot in their lives. Some stories of achievement, some of tragedy and hurt. I listen and it feels a privilege at times to hear others speak so intimately to me.

Now I enjoy these dates. I think I'm a good

listener. I learn that there are certain topics of conversation that are covered with each first date and after time develop a script that is carefully shaped.

My guide to First dates:

1. Do not start with your relationship history. This could scare some people off. It is accepted to cover this subject, but after an hour of the conversation and once you have built a rapport with them.

2. Start with an anecdote about something that has recently happened to you. Maybe on the way to the date or within your week. Nothing negative though, no one wants to sit there listening to you bitch or moan about something. Save that for after you've put a ring on their finger.

3. Always remember good eye contact and active listening skills. To show you are listening make sure you do plenty of nodding, uuhhs, ask some questions, reflection, and summary, but not too much, you do not want them to think they are being interviewed or on a counselling couch.

4. Do not go to the cinema. You are just sitting there waiting for the film to start in silence, or you are watching a film in silence. This is for established couples. You are not there

yet.

5. Active dates are best. This is why having Raff is so great as you can go for a walk, and then if it goes well grab a coffee or beer afterwards, and if it is not going well, you explain that he is overtired so you best get back otherwise he will play up. Sorry Mike, I used that excuse on you. Borrow a friend's dog if you must.

6. Talk about your work, but not too much as this can border on being boring. However, if you do something interesting or are passionate about what you do, then you need to share this.

7. Jokes are good. Clever people are funny. Fact. Use this quality if you have it.

8. Share your interests and hobbies. You will come alive, and the conversations will be more natural if you are talking about things that you are genuinely interested in.

9. Share your ambitions. If you do not have any then make something up. You do not want to come across as lazy.

10. Lastly, make sure you brush your teeth. Bad breath; not the best first impression. Oh, and wear something nice too, like my mum says, first impressions count.

Despite being accustomed to the fine tunes of dating, and from the list you would think I was an expert, but I rarely get second dates and most of the men still just want to have sex. This is not a road I want to visit again. No, it's not. I'm telling you. I want to leave some mystery after that first date and have them wanting more. I decide if all they are after is a quick shag, then they are not the ones for me. Good for you, Jonathan. For the next couple of months, most of my weekends are spent dating. It's my new hobby.

Michael – Time is running out

I must confess; I recognised Michael as the weatherman from the local news which influenced my decision to go on a date. He is a highly intelligent man, probably too intelligent for me as I am not political and do not watch the news. I was surprised by the fact that I knew him for being on the telly. I live in a bubble, it's great, come and join me. He does not hide the fact that he is gay, but I did still feel there was a conflict in him being able to freely be himself. He had previously been married to a woman which ended before him trying cock. It was odd people coming up to him and speaking to him as if he knew them. I think people thought I was his son as there was a bit of an age gap between us. He did tell me that most people in media are not very confident deep down, which I found interesting. 'They are all a bag of nerves back stage.' He was a real family man which was an incredibly endearing quality about him.

We walked around for a good few hours as we spoke about relationships, politics – I nodded and gave plenty of uuhhs at that point, growing up, family and aspirations. He would have made a very good mentor for me, I think. Actually, would he? Despite the extra years he had on me, he probably wasn't any wiser when it came to relationships or self-awareness. I think this highlights the complexities when it comes to dating.

There was a slight sadness to him, he was searching for love and had not found it, and I think he was worried he would run out of time. 'I would not change my life as it has given me the family I adore and a career I am proud of, but I do wish I realised who I was sooner.'

Mike – Don't call me, I'll call you

This was one of my more unfortunate dates. He seemed Chatty Cathy in text exchanges and when he spoke on the phone, but in person there was just nothing there. I'm not used to carrying a conversation but I did, really well I have to say, but he kept giving one word answers. Then he had this really nervous laugh. We exhausted all topics of conversation, in the end the only one I could think of was, 'so what you having for your tea then?' I wanted the ground to swallow me up and eat me whole. Or better still, for the ground to swallow him up. I'm sure he was a lovely guy whose nerves got the better of him. From what he was saying, in work he must be successful. He had a good car, but not a great deal of dress sense to be honest. I would have liked to take him shopping and introduce him to slim fit jeans as I'm sure he had a good physique hiding beneath those ill-fitting chinos and oversized tee.

I cannot recall a certain moment, phase or anecdote that is worthy of sharing. My date with Mike just highlighted that connection, or chemistry, is just not there with certain people. And nor should it be, I guess, otherwise it would not be special when it is there. It's a formula I'm yet to work out. There does not seem to be any science as to why we click with some people and not others. I think appearance and looks do have something to do with it, but I don't think it is just down to those things alone. Maybe having the same eyes as each other helps? Whatever it is, it was missing with Mike.

Jarrad – Avocados and Pears

I wanted to marry Jarrad. He was about 6'4 but carried his height with a matching muscular physique, and he was a dog lover too. He was obsessed by them and loved Raff. Probably more than me. He worked in production but had an ambition to quit his job, open a doggie day care business and have afternoon naps on giant bean bags with them all scattered on top of him. I wish

I was scattered on top of him. He was smart, passionate, and articulate and a greatly confident man who towered over me as he walked. If Barbie's Ken was modelled on anyone it would be Jarrad. I wish there was a second date, the first one went well. For me anyhow. I think I was just not his type, and that's okay. I am learning this. A few years ago, I would have been obsessed in thinking what did I do wrong, but I did not do anything wrong, we were just not compatible. I live in hope that Jarrad has a twin brother though, one with a filthy sexy mind and a passion for retired twinks.

Rupert – Love hurts

I met Rupert for a few drinks in town one Sunday afternoon.

Jonathan – Here already but don't rush. I am just outside Better Foods.

Rupert – 2 minutes away.

Jonathan – Okay great.

As I see him approach me, I can see he is a handsome and well put together man. Gym fit, tick. Good dresser, tick. On giving him a hug however I pick up on slight awkwardness which I interpreted as his disappointment in me not being what he expected. I think my photos now are too good and I don't live up to them. I knew this would happen and I was better as a pleasant surprise. Our conversation does flow, he probably talked more than me though. He's a highly successful businessman, owed to the fact that he spends copious amounts of time at work. It felt as though he likes to be in control which was on the one hand is sexy, but not sure how equal a partnership with him would be? He could have been in control in the bedroom, happy with that, but my fear would be what happens in other rooms, I would be on his arm as he navigates through his ambitions and aspirations for life. I don't want to be that guy.

He had money and having this lifestyle appeared important to him. Did I match this? Would I have been good enough? I don't think I would have been. I don't mean this in an arrogant way, but I think he saw himself as an A lister, myself a C lister (if that).

Tragically he lost his long-term partner eight years ago in an accident, so I think whoever he meets is not going to replace the love he lost. I found this really saddening. 'We were on a packed beach and I can remember looking around and seeing all these beautiful people on the beach and the one person I fancied, the only one person I had eyes for was him. Now how many people can say that?'

William – Just animal sex

A week later I have a moment of weakness. As you know I'm not doing hook ups, just dates, but one Sunday afternoon after a quiet day at home I find myself chatting to William who suggests meeting up. We had been exchanging the odd message throughout the week and whilst doing so I kept thinking he was not really my type, but I'm still in the mood for experimenting. He's this big burly bear at 6'5 tall and when I say hairy, I mean, unbelievably hairy. He was completely covered in hair, more of a gorilla than a bear thinking about it. I didn't see him as boyfriend material, but I was still fascinated by him. Is this what I'm looking for? A boyfriend? I don't know if this is what I desire. I'm starting to enjoy single life again. Anyhow, I'm straying again, I was turned on by talking to him, so I accepted his offer.

This is the other thing I like about hooking up. You get to see people's houses. Whilst chatting, I'm picturing William in his home. He's outside in the garden pulling vast weeds and brambles up with his bare hands with mud streaks on his face. He's wearing wellington boots and thigh hugging shorts and a tight fitted t shirt with the sleeves cut away. His house is a cabin with lots of natural woods and there is always a roaring fire lit. I now get to see how accurate I was. It wasn't a cabin, just a regular house, sparsely furnished and although nice, not a huge amount of style to it. Heck, I've just realised I'm quite judging, aren't I? He was very well spoken though which I was not expecting, and he was tall. He stood at his doorway and invited me in, this giant of a man towering over me.

We go up to his bedroom where we start kissing. I knew from our message exchanges he had some kinks. I think you would describe him as a Power Top. He liked edging and breath control and he described himself as enjoying dom sex. This still appeals to me, not in the way that Stuart wanted to play, but in a raw animal passion such as having sex with a bear or a gorilla. He delivered. There were moments where I felt like a fly caught in a spider's nest and I was his pray ready to be eaten. He did kind of eat me too. It was a cross between a love bite, which I haven't had since being fifteen when Kerrie Pinker gave me one on my neck at the end of a school disco, and an actual bite. He did this all over my body and particularly around my hips which I found very ticklish which turned him on and encouraged more. He seemed to love holding my waist with his massive hands which made me look so slim and small in comparison to him. I think he was turned on by this too. The sheer magnitude of him as he powered over me, I had no choice but to give myself to him.

The groping continued. That's not all that accurate of a word, it was more than groping, it felt good. We would kiss passionately too and every so often he would trap my tongue in his mouth. I'm not entirely sure how he did this, with his mouth I guess? He would then just hold me in this position until it was difficult for me to breath. Then just as he saw I was struggling, he would release me. Oh, and he had this amazing technique for playing with my penis. He cupped my balls firmly in one hand, as he wet his finger and rubbed the tip of my head quite firmly. I had not had that done to me before. I think I had an organism as he did this.

Clearly this just dating and not kissing the guy has not been all that successful. I decide I can't plan this, so as out of my comfort zone does it feel, I'm just going to go with the flow. I'm going to see what happens.

I have also been thinking what the headlines of my life would be to others. On a good day this might be, 'New lease of life – the adventures begins! On a bad day this would be, 'Desperado – he's back on the dating game! Now take a minute and just reflect for a bit, what is the headline of your life?

Chapter 19

Listen

It's coming up to five months now and I cannot believe I'm still thinking of Adam to the extent I am. At what point am I through a break up? Is there a set time? I'm still describing myself as recently single, but I don't know when I'll become just single. I guess when I feel completely over him. What is it about him? We were only together for two years, not twenty years. It doesn't feel I've moved on at all. I still torment myself with imagining him with other guys. Now he's not doing hook ups or group sex, but he's settled down with Hank. They love lazy Sunday mornings, they've already got in-jokes which only they get, they pee in front of each other (to be fair Adam always did that, he has this weird thing about not closing the door) and are generally just loved up. Meanwhile I'm just here.

I decide I cannot continue to think of Adam in this way anymore. I need to move on. I cannot have this conversation with Adam in person, so I write a letter which I later bin.

Dear Adam,

It has now been five months and I think of you daily, sometimes hourly. I don't fully understand why this is, but I know it has to stop. When we first met, I thought you were the one. I allowed myself to dream about our future together and pictured us one day living in the countryside or seaside surrounded by fresh air, nature and a pack of fur brothers which would be our family and home. But with everything that has gone on, the hurt we have put upon ourselves, our world can never be filled with fresh air, but fog and pollutants. This is the great loss for me. When we set out things felt perfect. Overtime this changed.

I've felt so many different feelings these past months. I go from anger, to hurt, to sadness to love. The mixture of these emotions is too much for me to take. I cannot and will not continue in this vein. You often accused me of being too quiet. I've been portrayed as this mysterious man who does not let you in. This is probably accurate. I don't know why my voice could not be heard within our relationship. I take ownership of this. I should have been stronger at the start. I have my voice back now.

There is part of me that feels used by you. When you were selling your house and struggled in your living situation, my ways were not an issue. It was not until you got a place of your own and gained confidence in your independence that my quietness became a problem. And during this time, I fell in love with you, causing these feelings of hurt and betrayal.

I could see your vulnerability when we first met, god I can still see it now. I took on this caring role for you. I think this accounts for me being stuck. I continue to care for you, even though you choose not to be part of my life. I think it's fair to say that you accepted this care when you needed it, but now you don't, and this is stifling for us both. I'm conflicted in being able to enjoy the good times we had as I question your sincerity. I think deep down you did love me, so I'm going to accept this and be grateful for those times, and for the learning that has taken place within, and after, our relationship.

This leaves me with one thing to do. I can no

longer grieve for you, I can no longer love and care for you, there will be no new adventures and no new dreams that we create. I need to let you go. Goodbye special man, it was a magical two years despite the hurt and pain we placed on each other. I hope you find the happiness with someone which you were unable to find with me.

Love and affection, Jonathan x

Chapter 20

Family holiday

The phone rings. It's my landline which means it's my mum. She's the only person to ring me on this phone.

'Hello.'

'Hi, love it's me, is now a good time?'

'Yes, it's fine, are you okay?'

'Yes, I've been speaking to your sister, and we think we all deserve a holiday so we have booked an apartment in Marseille for next month.'

'Whose we?'

'All of us. You, me, Joanna, your dad, and the

girls.'

'Together?'

'Yes together.'

'All of us?'

'Yes all of us.'

'Is that wise?'

'Your dad has paid for the accommodation, we just need to pay for the flights.'

'We've not been away together as a family for over twenty-five years. Can we manage being under the same roof?'

'Of course, it'll be fun.'

That word again, fun. I hear this term a lot on Grindr. It doesn't necessarily mean fun then and I'm not convinced that it will be fun here either. I cannot think of a valid excuse so bonjour France! A week away would actually be good for me. Although I feel like I'm starting to move on and feel more confident, the past few months have been bloody tough so a week lounging by the pool or on the beach does sound quite tempting. I think we won't need to do everything together right, and even if I only manage to carve out a few days by myself, it'll still be worth it.

***

It's four am and we are at the airport. I usually travel light with just hand luggage but my sister has three massive bags and a buggy to check in and that is the girl's stuff alone. The queue is long, and my mind can't help but wonder over the other passengers. I say wonder, maybe judge is a more appropriate word. How can some people just have no dress sense? They have mirrors in their houses, right? So many oversized baggy cargo shorts with clashing colours rather than accent or complimentary ones. Feet and legs that look like they haven't seen daylight in fifty years yet the owners of them still feel justified to expose them to the world. Sun hats that are so historical on the right person would be retro but, on these people, just so, so wrong. I like to make an effort when going on a flight. I like to convey an image of this jet setting international traveller. I'm wearing an emerald green, white and black stripped short sleeve shirt with a French tuck and looking so on trend, or so I think. I was, however, greeted by my sister singing Copacabana to me when she first saw me, but what does she know? My family and I seem normal compared to these people. In fact, my parents are actually quite trendy.

My dad, like the other men in the queue over sixty, is wearing shorts and sandals but his are at least straight cut and at the right length for his height. He's wearing a button-down shirt. Oh, but he does need a haircut though. He's had the same style for the past thirty odd years. It's modelled on Rob Steward and Keith Richards, his two style icons. He goes quite regularly to an expensive hairdresser but always comes out looking the same as when he went it. He refuses to wear product for some reason. Just a little bit would help. He is generally a very mellowed and chilled man. Well, apart from when his temper goes in which case, he does just lose it. This was never directed at me growing up as I was rarely naughty, but my sister did test boundaries at times so saw the raft of this anger. But as age sets in, so has slowness and this chilled lassez -faire attitude. Despite my dad physically being very fit and active, he's just so slow with everything he does. He literally crawls along like a snail, whereas I'm marching away. We are very different in this way. Already I'm feeling frustrated by his slowness.

I sometimes question whether I am a disappointment to him. I was this weedy, camp kid growing up who was crap at sports (well apart from netball, I can proudly boast that I was in the reserve netball team alongside my best friend Michael Fearne) and favoured shopping and baking over, well whatever most boys growing up in the 80s did; ride bikes or jump in rivers and other dirty activities. There was one time when I was fifteen, I had to call for him to remove a grasshopper from the kitchen. I thought it was an alien creature that I had discovered and feared it eating me. Despite this, he says he's proud of me, he always writes that in birthday and Christmas cards, but I struggle to accept it. The other day I rang him and he was watching the Lions and I had to guess if this was Football or Rugby. I did guess right but it was a fifty percent chance of getting this wrong and just highlights our differences.

While I'm describing my family, here is my mum. What can I say about my mother? Okay she is lovely. Appearance wise she is very petite and very glamourous. She would never leave the house or answer the front door without lipstick on, or full make up come to that. I remember when she was diagnosed with fibromyalgia her doctor wanted her to go onto steroids which she point blank refused as she feared putting on weight. 'I know what will happen, my face will get fat and my feet will go all puffy,' she cried. That was over eight years ago and she would still rather be in pain than have a fat face. I think I get my sense of style from her. She's been single twenty odd years as she refuses to use dating apps as she sees it as desperation. Well, she's right there and is probably going to have a shock when she sees my use of them. Oh fuck, that's going to be awkward. I can't see my mum ever meeting anyone. I don't think she'll be able to compromise in living with anyone but herself. She has a very set way of doing things, everything has a place so any movement away from this feels impossible. When I visit, I hear, 'why are these keys here?' or 'whose shoes are these?', or 'are you going to put your bags in your bedroom?'

I diligently ring my mum twice a week; Wednesdays and weekends. We easily find things to chat about and I like our phone calls, but there are times when she will come across as quite negative. I think living on your own for so long there is no one to chat through problems with so these get stored up for me and perceived by her as of greater importance than what they really are. Have I got this to look forward to? Am I my mother where I'll be single for the next twenty odd years? 60 still Single still Gay. I am set in my ways too. I've only just become aware of this revelation. Ponders.

My sister, she is recently single too after splitting up with husband and the father of her two children. Although my sister is two years older than me, I have always felt like her older brother, for some reason. Academically she was bright, and this felt a pressure growing up trying to match her which I never achieved. We've never been that close, but I know she is always there for me if I need her. We share the same humour, but I think that might be all we share. Our outlook on life is completely different. She is a constant worrier, whereas I tend not to worry about things outside my control. Joanna will also obsess about things. I think we've learnt that I might do that too, but I do not worry.

Oh, and my nieces too. Okay I'll share a secret with you. There is part of me that resents them. There I said it. Not only does that make me a bad uncle, but it makes me a bad person too. I've always been the youngest one in our family, often the centre of attention. This went when Joanna had her first child. All of a sudden everything was focused on her. I also don't like children, which I think I alluded to in an earlier chapter. It's the unpredictability of them. Also, what's with the assumption that everyone is interested in the so-called cuteness of a baby. My sister doesn't do this at least, but friends who constantly post pictures of their children doing nothing but sit there looking chubby. I don't actually care. Although to be fair to my nieces, they do come out with some funny things and they adore Raff so perhaps I'm starting to soften to them, just a smidgen.

Despite getting to the airport three and a half hours prior to the flight – that was Joanna's influence as she was worried we would miss it – we do in fact nearly miss our flight. I'm not sure how exactly. Everything takes ten times longer with children. There is so much more to think about. Add the snail's pace of my dad into this mix and it's a bad combination. I try to explain that it was the last call but he was convinced they wouldn't leave without him as if he really is Rod Stewart. Reality check dad, you're not and it's an EasyJet flight. We do, however, just make it in time and I'm greeted to the sound of screaming children and those badly dressed people I saw earlier.

I sit next to my nieces, I don't know why but they are obsessed with sitting next to me. I'm a miserable bastard, Granny and Gramps will be much more fun, but no 'I'm sitting next to Uncle Jonathan.' 'Me too I want to be next to Uncle Jonathan.' I was sandwiched between them, and this admiration didn't just last the flight.

We arrive in Marseille, and I can't wait to get off the plane and shake the chavy people whose air I had been breathing off me. As I leave, I'm hit by the sun. I absolutely love that feeling. Of course, it's too hot for Joanna and the girls who are already complaining of the heat. This continues for the duration of the holiday. My dad starts to haggle with a local taxi driver for a cheap rate to our apartment. That's another comparison I can make with my dad, he's a bit of a Del Boy at times. The ride we end up with is definitely not a registered taxi but just some local with a saloon car which amazingly we manage to squeeze into. I thought the flight was bad. There's no air con in the car or suspension for that matter, we feel every bump in the road and the apartment turns out to be quite a way from the airport. We do finally make it there.

The apartment is lovely with gorgeous views over a square and harbour which I just adore.

Already Joanna and I have reverted to being teenagers again as we argue over which rooms we are going have. How the hell are we going to cope being under the same roof for a whole week? The girls are just running excitedly from room to room jumping on the bed and, oh what? Someone's done a fucking shit on the floor in my bedroom.

'Joanna, there's a poo on my floor.'

'What?'

'Someone has done a poo right in the middle of my bedroom.'

As Joanna cleans the poo my mum reaches for the booze as my dad has a fag on the balcony. I join him. I'm painting quite a picture of them. I do actually love them dearly. That's one of the nice things of smoking at the moment. I have something in common with my dad. Probably the only thing.

'Hey dad.'

'Have one of these if you like?'

'I'm fine with a roll up, prefer them. The view is beautiful isn't it, I love seeing the water.'

'Yeah me too, so relaxing. Everyone else okay?'

'Yeah they're good, although Lexy did a poo in my room.'

My dad sniggers. Our conversations don't really go beyond this. I know there's love there even if we don't say it. Or show it. Whereas Joanna and my dad have much more in common; they both follow sports, watch the same comedy shows, both watch Top Gear and whatever that other one is called. I'm more like my mum. Everyone says it and I guess it's true. Both into fashion and style, both can be quite judgemental at times, same observational humour. There is an old lady begging on the square pretending she has a bad back, like really bad back. She's so hunched over it is clearly a scam as occasionally we see her go behind a pillar to have a fag and stretch her back out. For some reason mum and I find this hilarious and our whole time whilst on holiday is spent watching her and seeing all the people she scams out of loose change.

We soon discover that the air con is broken. I can deal with this, but my sister can't. I swap rooms with her as apparently mine is slightly better, but this is not enough and the first two days of the holiday is spent by all of us swapping rooms, trying to get an engineer to fix it, followed by eventually moving apartments. I knew this would happen, already this holiday is feeling like hard work.

The holiday continues in this vein with the days focused around what the girls want to do. I know, I'm a fully grown adult, of course the holiday will be focused on them. We go to the beach but whereas my idea of the beach is relaxing for a few hours in the sun, a couple of cold beers, a few trips to the water to cool off, then more cooking in the sun. This beach trip is sand castles, swimming with my nieces, being buried in sand and made into a mermaid and listening to Lexy have a tantrum because she didn't want to share a sun lounger with her mum. Now when I say tantrum, I mean she really went for it. Joanna had to walk away as she found it quite difficult, which was fine, but it did mean the whole beach thought that Lexy was my child and were looking at me in horror as she cried and screamed and kicked her legs in rage, whilst I tried to ignore her and drink my beer.

There is something quite freeing about how a child reacts. I would say, fifty odd people at least could hear her screams, but she didn't give one fuck. At what point in life do we develop that self-consciousness that stops us from doing what we want? Is it social norms, where over time we learn how we should behave and what we should say? Or is it more internalised than this?

Would I do anything differently if I could? I might have responded to Adam's mum's passive aggressiveness. Bitch. Maybe I would have been less prudish in my teenage years and explored my sexuality earlier. I'm struggling to think of much more I would do differently. I guess that's a good thing.

Back to the relaxing day on the beach. Lexy does eventually stop crying after half an hour or so after being bribed by an ice cream. I get one too so

I'm not going to make any parenting comments. We stroll back to the apartment where we all flop to our rooms for a sleep apart from my mum whose looking to get the party started by cracking open a bottle of sparkly. I think of Raff, I miss him. He's with his Aunty Fliss so I know he'll be fine. I think of Adam still, I miss him too. He's with Hank so he's probably being buggered to an inch of his life. Hank has no issue with his erection. He doesn't get caught up into his head trying to analyse the other person's feelings or thoughts, he's much more simplistic in his thinking.

I'm not used to spending so much time with my family and in a perverse way I'm starting to enjoy it. I no longer feel that I've reverted to being a teenager but now I've taken on the parental role! I'm usually the responsible one in most situations. I think it came from when my parents separated when I was eleven, and I remember my mum telling me I was the man of the house now. I don't think she realised what she was saying, and at the time I don't think I consciously felt the gravity of that statement, but I wonder if sub consciously I took on that as a level of responsibility. It has its advantage, I'm great in an emergency situation, but equally is this why I'm not spontaneous, or fun and why I'm boring? Actually, I'm not boring. I'm funny and starting to be more expressive.

I do carve out a small amount of time for

myself. I go running. Despite my smoky lungs they manage to carry me for some early morning runs where I feel alive. Whilst running I'm able to allow my thoughts to just be and I'm sure there must be endorphins or something which are released as I always feel better for it. I feel good about myself, which I should. I'm a good person. Recently whilst on a first date someone described Raff and I as 'good souls.' I like that. One morning, ridiculously early, as I couldn't sleep, I got up and went for a run. No one was around and so I went down to the water's edge, completely stripped and immersed myself in the water. I floated and felt at one with the world as I looked up to the beautiful sky above and looked down into the clean, crisp water below and I felt a connection to both elements. I think I'm starting to heal.

***

Later that morning, my dad hires a car so we can explore further afield. Okay, road trip! He doesn't allow anyone else but him to drive. I'm a good driver but for some reason he does not trust me. I am in charge of the music though and my songs are on shuffle as we get completely lost along a road. Oh yeah, I'm in charge of directions too which is not my forte. As we drive along Do-Re-Me, from the Sound of Music, plays. Really cool, I know. I start singing and am joined by my nieces, followed by my mum, then Joanna and then even my dad joins in. It is a beautiful moment that I will cherish. We became the Von Trap Family. For that moment I fit in.

Chapter 21

Baz

I was pleasantly surprised to receive a message from Baz about a month after we met in his hotel room. As you know I gave him my number and we intermittently exchanged the odd text but this soon fizzled out. It was about 5pm and I was at the gym. He was on the train and would be staying near to me.

'Fancy coming around?' he asked.

I instantly replied back. Really good at playing it cool there, Jonathan. 'Yes I'd be up for that.'

We arranged for me to go around there for 8pm so I eagerly cut my gym session short to get ready. I don't know why but I struggled to sleep the previous night so I have a quick snooze, followed by a bath (appropriate I know) in order to freshen up. Only trouble is, I still feel absolutely shattered. Dating is tiring. Trying to transform my body and keep this shit up is tiring. I message him back.

Jonathan – Hey there. I'm still up for coming around but have to confess to feeling absolutely shattered. Didn't sleep well last night, then gym, snooze and bath has made me feel sleepy. Can't promise an intense night of passion, but happy to go for a drink or just hang out in your hotel room, if you are up for that? Understand if you would rather pass and we could always meet up next time you are in the city.

Baz – Hi Jonathan. I feel the same! Why don't you come round and let's see what happens.

Jonathan – Yes sure thing. See you later.

Just before I leave, I get an email from Adam. He tells me that he misses me. You would have thought I'd jump at the chance of getting back with him but I'm left asking what's changed? If I wasn't enough then, what makes me enough now? I spend time articulating my response only for Adam to find fault and start accusing me of 'never being enough for him and hating his flat'. I didn't see it then but writing it now I think that's projection right? As his original feeling towards me was that I was not enough. Anyway, I don't have time to think about it now.

I arrive to find Baz sitting on a park bench opposite the hotel in which he is staying. He seemed less confident than when I last met him and had a suppressed energy to him. I sit next to him, and we smoke our cigerallos. I am cutting down, well sometimes, but do still enjoy them. I feel almost ready to let them go. The conversation still flows. I think I see the real him on that bench. In fact, I think I also saw the real him a few weeks before and he has multiples sides to his personality. As we all do, I guess. Look at me whoring it up before, a side of me I keep hidden to most. What am I trying to say? I'm not sure exactly. There was a sadness to him. We speak in a real way not trying to impress each other, which I'm finding most people do whilst dating, but there was transparency to his words.

Back at the hotel room I make a cup of tea for us both. Last time I visited him I had lube and condoms stuffed in my pockets, tonight I have a sandwich bag with some earl grey tea bags. I sit next to him on his bed and we continue to talk about his day and the impact travelling has on him. I learn he sold his house and just sleeps in hotel rooms. I don't ask but I wonder where he does his laundry. I glanced across at his suitcase. It is tiny. I'm a home bird. I get home sick on holidays at times, I don't think I could do that.

As we talk he occasionally strokes my leg. It's a pleasing sign that he is interested in me, but I am still not feeling very sexual. Instead, I nestle into his arm and lay my head into his shoulder. We stay there in silence until I speak .

'Is this weird?'

'No, not at all. Well it might be weird because it doesn't happen all the time but it's nice.'

'So you don't have a house? I'm not sure if I could live without having a place I come back to.'

'I think about my flat and how much I loved it, I had spent time over the years getting it just as I wanted, but I was never there so I just sold it. I made a lot of money on it as it was in central London. Of course, its quadrupled in price since I sold it.'

'You don't miss it?'

'Sometimes I do yes.'

We talk about where he grew up, about his childhood. He has three siblings but is only in contact with one of them. His parents died some time ago.

'I see my little sis sometimes. We chat regularly too, but that's about it really.'

'Another cuppa?' I say as I go to put the kettle on again.

'Yeah that will be great.'

'And you really don't know where you'll be from one day to the next?'

'Not really, it all depends on the schedule and whether the director has fucked up another scene and we have to go back somewhere to reshoot. That's why I'm back here.'

We lay next to each other, I have one hand placed under his T-shirt on his stomach and we slowly drifted asleep. It's an exceptionally beautiful moment. I wake to darkness.

'I need to get back to Raff.'

'Okay,' he replies.

'No, don't get up, you stay there.'

I kiss him on the forehead as I leave.

'Good night Baz.'

'Good night Tarzan.'

***

It was about six weeks later when I was scrolling through Facebook one morning and he came up as a friend suggestion. I went into his profile to learn that he died only two weeks after I'd last seen him. He took his life. I only met him twice and exchanged the odd message over a month so I don't really know how I should respond to this. I do feel sad, there is a familiarity to those feelings of loss I felt for Adam.

After a quick internet search I find out that gay men are four times more likely to take their life than a heterosexual man. Yet I don't see any campaigns raising awareness to this. I don't know if I should have done more. I mean, I know I only met him twice but when I saw him sitting on that bench, I questioned in my head if he was ok. Would it have made a difference if I had voiced that question aloud?

That night I buy a pack of cigerallos – I had been good the whole week – and on my balcony, I light one for him. I feel sad standing there as I think about him. I'm pretty sure there wouldn't have been a relationship there, and like I say I hardly knew him, so I don't feel a loss for me, but his loss. The loss of a life.

Chapter 22

Raff

My one true love is Raff. For years I looked at dogs for sale on an internet app. I would spend hours searching for different breeds of dogs; Pugs, Italian Greyhounds, Boston Terriers. This has now been replaced for searching for men on dating sites; Jocks, Muscles and Bears. Raff is the only dog who I called to enquire about. A few days later I went up to see him and ended up bringing him home with me there and then, and the rest is history. It was the best decision of my life not to listen my mum's advice, 'they're a tie, you can never go out, you'll never be able to go on holidays.' It does make these things a little trickier, but I was never a spontaneous person anyway. The unconditional love I feel for Raff outweighs any cheap last-minute getaway and Raff has been an absolute strength for the four years we have been together.

The breakup has been hard on Raff too. Like I say, he adored Adam. For the first month or even longer, come to think about it, he would look out the balcony waiting for the sound of Adam's car. 'He's not coming back,' I would tell him, but of course he did not understand. I do sometimes think it must be amazing to think the same way as a dog. Every day is an adventure. Apart from objects of reference they quickly learn, they have no idea of what is happening next. I can pick up his lead, but he doesn't know where we are going or who he might see. I might know that Fliss is going to pop around for a coffee, he loves her as he gets completely fussed over, but he does not know this until the doorbell rings. Life is so exciting for him. Although this not knowing can have its disadvantages too, such as learning you are not enough for someone. What was it, seventy percent perfect? Sorry I've let go, I wrote that letter and everything. I've also just completely contradicted myself in those two paragraphs. I'm not spontaneous, yet I want to be? What's that about?

I could easily add spontaneity to my life if I wanted.

With Adam gone, I notice that Raff is following me around, a lot. He did before to an extent but now I cannot go anywhere without him at my feet trying to trip me up at every turn. Even when I take a bath, he will jump up as if he is ready to dive in and then settle for the laundry basket where he will curl up on the clean clothes yet to be put away. At night when we watch TV, Raff will curl up on my lap and then looks up at me in a way I have not experienced from anyone else. It is complete admiration that he has for me. I'm not seventy percent perfect to him, I'm a full one hundred.

Raff is a complete foodie. Obsessed by it. I do struggle with this aspect of his personality, I just think it's a grotesque quality to have. He will often jump up at people if he knows there is food in their pockets. He did this to a lady in the park once who was far from impressed. 'Your dry-cleaning bill must be big as this is a designer coat.'

'I'm so sorry, he's not my dog I'm just looking after him for the day,' I replied as we sheepishly vacated the park.

Then another time whilst out with Fliss, who took him to a coffee shop, he swiped a fried egg from someone's plate. He was cute though so was able to get away with this. He had the whole coffee shop in hysterics.

He does have a stubborn streak though. He can be often heard grunting when I try to get him to do something that he does not agree too, I think this is the Pug in him. It also saddens me to say but if Raff had his own Grindr profile, his top hashtag would be scat. He is, however, extremely loveable and an absolute rock. On the night of the split, he knew that I was upset. On returning home he would not settle and just looked at me all puzzled and confused. He's always slept on my bed ever since he was a puppy. On the first night of getting him I tried to be disciplined and to get him to sleep in his basket on the floor. That lasted for one night before I caved to those big brown eyes. We are a pair, so if I do find love again it will need to be someone accepting of a fluffy mutt who often has bad flatulence and no filter for when this is executed.

My top 10 Raff moments:

1. Barry Island beach where Raff peed against a little boy's sandcastle which he had been so carefully constructing. Raff just tootled up to it and lifted his leg. The little boy's face was a picture as his dad and everyone else who witnessed the event couldn't help but laugh.

2. I think it was the same beach trip where he went over to a family picnic and ate a girl's

jam sandwich and licked a cookie. He was on a roll that day.

3. Another food related one when I took him to the office and he managed to open the biscuit jar, which was sealed Tupperware, and ate all the chocolate biscuits resulting in a trip to the vet where he had to have an injection to be sick. This confirmed just how precious he was to me.

4. Every morning we have a routine where I'll feed him, it gets earlier and earlier but we've settled on 6.30am, he'll then go back to bed. Then when it's walk time, he will refuse to get out of bed and roll over on his back with his legs in the air and I have to lift him off the bed. I don't know why he does this as I'm sure he really wants to go out. It's like a little game we play.

5. Once, when he was at Steve's during his puppy stage, he chewed his way through his wallet including notes and we came back to pieces of this scattered throughout the living room floor.

6. I nearly forgot about this, but he also chewed the back leather seats to Steve's new Audi RS3. Thanks Raff, I had to pay for those when Steve and I split up.

7. At night when he will curl himself in a ball and sit on my lap.

8. The bobbing head and look of disgust when

Adam and I were fooling around in bed must be a Top 10 moment. I have never seen a look like it. Well, maybe the sandcastle boy had a similar look.

9. When walking in fields with long grass he gets all frisky and will run in circles in this crazy fashion.

10. There is a certain look of affection he gives which has been unrivalled by anyone else I know. He's so adorable.

The advantage to having a dog, is that everyone is friendlier to you. Without Raff by my side, I would be invisible to the majority of passers-by. With Raff, people stop and chat. 'Oh look at him. He's adorable,' 'What's his name?' Or 'What is he?' I get that a lot. Then the bemusement when I explain his mixed breed of Shih-Tzu, Pug and Whippet. The funniest reply to this was some bloke who replied, 'a threesome was it?' It's as if because I'm loved by a dog, it makes me more acceptable to the rest of society. 'He can't be that bad, he's a dog lover.' I love this attention. I did, however, get jealous once at DogFest where Raff was side-lined for another dog. Then later I heard a little girl say, 'look mummy it's one of those dogs that look like a pig.' Bitch.

Most people, however, look at Raff and not me, so I don't think I'm going to attract a future mate in this way. Of the dates I do end up getting,

I'm totally eclipsed by him. I don't care though as I question how many dates were achieved from having him in the first place, and a dog walk as a first date is a more relaxed way of meeting someone for the first time.

I already get anxiety dreams about him dying. Tom and I used to have Chinchillas (extremely fluffy balls of cuteness). Whenever I was anxious or stressed, I would dream about them escaping and I would be trying to capture them but there would always be more to find. Now I imagine Raff has run off a cliff or eats something poisonous or is knocked over by a car. I already worry about what I'm going to do when he is no longer part of my life. I'm quickly moving on from that thought, as I have plenty of other morbid and depressing thoughts in my head, so let's get back to the misery that is my life.

Chapter 23

Understanding

'What did you get out of the relationship?' This is what my counsellor asked me. Yes I'm in counselling as I thought it would help with this feeling of being stuck. The letter clearly didn't work. Such a simple question but one that I struggle to answer. I don't know what to say. I go on to identify the caring role I took on. I felt like his carer. Is this why I struggle to let go? What did I get out of the relationship? I'm still not sure.

'Was it companionship?'

'You're asking me?' says my counsellor.

'I'm not sure. I think we met at a time when we needed each other. That first night felt magical. As if the universe had brought us together.'

'He was your first love?'

'Yes … in that way, yes. I hadn't really thought about it like that. I had a purpose with him.'

'A purpose, you feel you don't have one now?'

'I do, I am me, and I mostly like me. I liked looking after him, he didn't ask me too, but I think I became his carer to some degree. I could see his vulnerability from his past relationship. I wanted to help him.'

'You wanted to help him?'

'Yes, perhaps I liked being needed. Is this why I'm struggling with moving on, because the focus is me, and not him?'

'Is that your focus, because what I'm hearing is that he is still your focus?' Gill was of course right, the checking his status on apps, seeing if he was online, the constant thinking of how he was doing, even now I think of him and struggle to say good bye.

My counsellor, Gill, is a woman in her early fifties. She seems so grounded. She creates a safe space which, over time, I fill with my demons and slowly we make sense of them. The hurt and loss I feel, my obsessive behaviours, my relationship with Grindr and my fears for the future. Some of them go, others get smaller, where they seem less scary, and others stay where I accept them for me. Just by talking about them they make more sense. I'm also surprised by how I easily fill the space. I was worried I wouldn't have enough to say. I'm a quiet, quirky person who's always in their head, after all, but I do fill the space, and my thoughts and feelings are carefully held by Gill and passed back to me to accept, challenge or change. I only have six sessions, but it's enough to help me start to move on and refocus.

I understand my relationship with Grindr more. It's not about sexual gratification, very rarely does a meet fulfil me. It's a quest for intimacy which I have learnt is easier to give as sex than through friendship. If a hook up does not go well, I know I never need to see them again. If a chat goes south, I delete. I'm in control. There is also an element of liking the attention I get from Grindr, even though I know in my head how artificial it is. I'm representing myself through a small 1cm square tile and a few chosen words about how fitness, dogs and a healthy lifestyle is important to me. Even that's a lie as I'm still smoking.

My smoking gets explored too. They are not cancer sticks, they are my friends. When I am lonely or feel sad, I hold one, or it holds me. In the moment of having the cigarette I find relief. It's not escapism, if I don't want it to be. I can move into the feelings I am having and reflect if I want to, or not. I do need to stop.

I look at my obsessive behaviour. I know it's not normal. I ask the question, is it Adam I'm missing, or am I just lonely? I think it's the former. There were moments in our relationship where it felt perfect. Just simple things like talking in the kitchen whilst making a cup of tea after sex, going on a walk with Raff, cuddling on the sofa. I am yet to match those feelings with anyone, and this feels so far away. Memories and flash backs still visit me. If I go to a place where we visited, he is my first thought. If I see a food item on a menu we have had, he is my first thought. If a programme comes on that we watched together, he is my first thought. I often, sometimes constantly, imagine what he is doing. One of the main influencers for this is wanting to know if he is okay. When did I become his carer? Why am I still caring for him when he has made it clear he no longer wants this from me?

I've always taken on this carer role, not just with Adam but in life. I think it comes from the comment my mum made about being the man of the house when my mum and dad split up. That burden I felt as a young child has stayed with me. Don't get me wrong, I acknowledge it is a good quality to have, but it is also a heavy one. I need to learn to take care of myself which means letting go of Adam, I'm just not sure how yet.

My family get a mention whilst in counselling too. The holiday helped in making me recognise that I do form part of my family however I can't help but still feel very different to them. Perhaps I am? Perhaps that's okay. I'm able to see and accept the similarities and the differences. I look like my dad, I have things in common with my mum, I have my dad's work ethic, I have my mum's style, I have my sister's humour. I think very differently to all of them. I love them. They love me.

I realise that I need new experiences and a new focus. I start to create an ambitious list of fifty things to do before I'm fifty. I struggle to reach all fifty and I think I only chose this number because it has a nice ring to it, I do, however, come up with the following:

1) Design and make an outfit
2) Get high in Amsterdam
3) Be a Best man at a wedding
4) Become an expert in something
5) Climb Sydney Harbour Bridge
6) Climb Ben Nevis with Raff
7) Go on a road trip with my dad
8) Stay at Burgh Island Hotel
9) Go island hopping around Greece
10) Go to Glastonbury Festival
11) Buy a house with a garden

12) Go on a March (the cause doesn't matter)

13) Do some volunteering

14) Learn to speak a foreign language

15) Take part in a pub quiz

16) Do an anonymous good deed

17) Go shopping in Tokyo

18) Feature in a local Life magazine at some launch party holding a glass of champagne

***

A strange thing happened to me today. I was singing Belinda Carlisle's Heaven is a Place on Earth, I don't know why it just popped into my head. I then put on the radio and the song was playing. This also happened to me about eight years ago when I was singing an even more unusual song, One of Us by Joan Osbourne. I expect you might know it if you are the same generation as me, it features the lyric 'What if god was one of us, just a slob like one of us, just a stranger on the bus, trying to make his way home.' I know it from Joan of Arcadia, an American teen drama series in the early noughties where Joan sees God in different forms and helps with an assignment which usually involves saving someone's life. I'm digressing but they are such random songs, is it a coincidence that they happened to be on the radio whilst I was singing them. Or does it represent something else?

Adam used to say, the most plausible answer,

tended to be the correct answer, but what's plausible here? It feels so random that it was purely a coincidence. I could understand if I was singing a song which was currently number one in the charts and had a lot of airtime, but these songs, particularly the last one is hardly ever played. This makes me think, was I hearing the radio waves in some way? That's interesting though, because if the radio is not on, are they there? This is starting to sound like that mind puzzle you are told as a kid about the tree that falls with no one around, does it make a noise? Answers on a postcard please.

I can't also help but feel the significance of the lyrics. Is it a sign? There is a religious significance to both songs. I do not describe myself as a religious person, or a spiritual one for that matter. I was asked this recently on a date and didn't really know what to say. I believe, when you are dead, you are dead. That's it. No afterlife, no returning as ghosts, no reincarnation, our bodies just get reabsorbed into the ground. However, experiencing the song phenomenon for a second time I did start to question my deep-rooted beliefs in nothing. I do think there is more to our mind that we don't use when living and this leads onto my other explanation which is that I'm psychic or intuitive in some way. I've always felt I am good at reading emotions. Perhaps this is an extension of this? I also question how much of Adam's ambivalence I was picking up on when he would describe me as being in my head? I guess I'm never going to know. Odd though.

I've now got that song in my head. Sing with me...Ooh baby, do you know what's that worth? Ooh, Heaven is a place on Earth. They say in Heaven, love comes first...We'll make heaven a place on Earth.

C h a p t e r   2 4

Ethan

Meeting someone three times within one day is more than a coincidence, right? I first ran into him on my estate. I was walking Raff as he was walking out of the coffee shop come trendy restaurant opposite my building. He first spotted Raff, everyone does, then he spotted me. You can just tell if someone is into you. Their eyes speak and I definitely heard him as we glanced for just a few seconds but it was enough to feel a volt of energy run up and down my body. I said 'hi' and he returned with a 'hi' too. Love it Jonathan, keep it casual. He then continued to walk past me and I didn't think I would ever see him again.

Enter second meet. About two hours later I was at the supermarket buying my shopping for the week. I always buy the exact same items and have set meals on set days. Does anyone else do this or is it just me? I once tried buying other people's shopping for a while. I would look for a discarded shopping list or till receipt and buy the items of a stranger. You should try this. It's strangely liberating but you do end up with some crap at the end of the week. Once I brought the shopping of someone who I'll call Mrs Cheese. How she didn't have a heart attack whilst cruising the supermarket shelves from all the dairy she and her family consume is beyond me. Anyway, this week I was just buying my own shopping and as I was about to unload, oh sounds a bit sexual in a very nonsexual way, my items at the till point that same guy was there. He was only buying three items so I said to him he could go in front of me.

'Are you sure?'

'Yes, that's fine go ahead.'

'You're an angel, thank you so much.'

I've never been called an angel before, not by a stranger or a man even. I felt chuffed with my angelic stature. As he passed me along the narrow aisle I say, 'just be careful of my wings.' We smiled simultaneously. We shared a moment.

Our third encounter was at the gym. We arrived pretty much at the same time. We spotted each other amongst a back drop of bright lights, gym equipment, high beat music and a scattering of people working out. I initiated our conversation, 'Hello again, are you following me?'

He giggled, slightly nervously. 'It would appear so.'

'I've not seen you here before.' Cheesy line I know.

'You wouldn't have, I've just moved to the area, I'm Ethan.'

'Hi Ethan, I'm Jonathan.'

Let me spend some time describing Ethan. He's very handsome. I would guess he is in his late twenties, so far too young for me. Jet black hair which I can see poking out of the baseball cap he is wearing backwards on his head. Now really, he's probably too old for wearing a backwards baseball cap but he's able to pull it off. He looks a bit American, a little bit like Clarke Kent but younger. He has that sporty, geek thing going on. He has piercing, bright blue eyes and some stubble on his face. He's hot. He's wearing a muscle vest which shows off his strong arms as well as his V shape body and I count four prominent ribs, which I want to lick. I love him already. He's a bit shorter than me. He has the most amazing smile with big white teeth which match mine. I feel myself blush as I talk to him. For goodness sake Jonathan, you're forty now.

'Well enjoy your workout,' he says to me as he jumps onto the cross trainer and puts his ear phones in. This was the end of our conversation. I know, it's still very brief but it is a start. I try not to obsess too much about him, but I can't help myself. I always think when we meet someone we like, there must be one or two qualities that come together to create that volt of energy like I had earlier outside the coffee shop. I guess I'm describing attraction and isn't it beautiful that we all see different qualities in different people making a diverse tapestry for each of us to shine. I'm not sure exactly what qualities I saw in Ethan that I was attracted to, but there was something. Now I'm not sure if you do this but once I've found someone who I'm attracted too I'll start creating an image in my head of who I think they are then over time they either live up to this image – he's then a keeper – or slowly begin to disappoint where I learn he's allergic to dogs and he chews with his mouth open and does drugs or something.

For now, Ethan is perfect. He is a dog lover, he runs and does yoga daily. That's how he starts his day. He drinks strong black ground coffee. He's funny too, so funny. He's really quick witted and has a very dry sense of humour. What else can I tell you about him? He has a good job, I don't understand exactly what he does but he's very clever. That's right, he's an engineer, but he's not geeky like a lot of his co-workers. I start to notice his kindness and gentle soul. It's amazing that he can switch from being the life and soul of the party and carry the complete room, to showing this deep emotional connection. Obviously, this is all in my head.

Over the next few weeks we continue to see each other at the gym. We don't talk but just the occasional nod and smile. I want to talk to him, but I keep stopping myself. Then one day whilst I was using the big functional trainer machine thing, you know the one with the ropes and you can put different attachments on it, he asked if I was using both sides. 'No that's fine,' I tell him.

'So how are you getting on here, you enjoying the gym?' Face slap. Enjoying the gym? Why would I ask him that?

He replies, 'Yes, it's a good gym. Much bigger than other ones I have gone to.'

Our conversation continues. I ask him why he moved here. He goes on to tell me that he was in the army but has since left. Of course, with those arms. I learn that he grew up in this area and decided to return. He's now training to become a PT but works at another gym. Again, I knew this. I want to marry him. It was quite refreshing, I didn't tell you before but Ethan had started to become my new obsession. Maybe you worked that out? I would think about him daily, well nightly to be more accurate. I would plan my gym visits to when I thought he would be there. I would imagine us in everyday scenarios like cuddling up on the sofa or taking Raff for a walk. Now I'm probably oversharing.

'You've got good technique he tells me.'

You've not seen me in the bedroom I think. 'Aww, thanks.' He asks me what I do and we continue to talk for what feels the night. In reality it was a ten-minute conversation. I leave the gym feeling good. Still no closer to a date though. I don't even know if he is gay, but a straight guy wouldn't call anyone an angel would they? Heck, if Ethan read this book he wouldn't be calling me an angel then, a horny devil more like. I once got a tattoo of a Tasmanian devil. Just what was I thinking? I was only eighteen and felt under pressure to choose a design so just went with that. It's been covered up now. There is definitely an attraction there which I'm almost certain is shared.

I'm not sure how or when it happened but we started working out together. One time he was showing me a particular back work out, and we just moved around the gym from equipment to equipment. It felt like a dance. Then I just went for it.

'Do you want to grab a drink after this?'

'Sure why not.'

This was the beginning. I had already started to learn about him through our gym sessions, but over a drink, I got to see the real him. I found his mind rather than just his arms. I struggled to picture him in the army, but this formed part of his past, and maybe some of the mystery. From our first drink we move to our first meal to what I'm calling our first date. We started to go to the gym together as a routine. We went to the cinema. We chatted at ease, we laughed at the same things. I could see he was into me but after a month we hadn't even kissed. What was this? Was it purely a friendship?

I regularly chatted to Fliss about whether I should tell him how I feel. I didn't want to mess up a friendship, but equally my time spent away from him was becoming unmanageable. I would feel sick when not with him. I think there is something wrong with me. I have an obsessive personality. I don't know if that's going to change. Oh well, might as well accept it. Fliss was convinced he was straight, that if something was to happen then it would have by now. 'Don't do it, you'll just mess up a friendship and feel bad about yourself.'

'He's never mentioned a girlfriend before.'

'That means nothing, have you talked about boyfriends?'

'Well, no.'

A disapproving 'hmmm' followed.

I was never good at following advice. I have a strong mind. I never accept a compliment, but at the same time I never take on criticism. And guess what? Turned out I was right. I thought I needed to get the setting right for him to truly express himself. It cannot be anywhere in public, so I invited him for food back at mine following a gym session. It was a leg day. It was salmon, broccoli and some rice. I know I'm still on the eating healthy train, it's hell. It was a Thursday. I love Thursday, my favourite day. It was also an amazing first kiss. It led to more.

Chapter 25

Romance

There is a frailty when having sex with someone you care about for the first time. With the casual encounters on Grindr I feel in control. I know it's probable that I'm not going to see them ever again and that's very liberating. With Ethan this feels like a make-or-break situation. I've never been all that body confident and that feeling of being naked and dumped has stayed with me. I do, however, know that I need to take risks if I want to move on and Ethan feels like a risk I want to take.

As we kiss passionately our hands move up and down each other's body. His skin feels very smooth, it's like he's got oily skin, but not in a greasy way. He's mostly smooth apart from a small triangle of hair on his immaculately formed chest. Initially we kiss with our eyes closed but I open mine as I want to see what is happening and shortly after he does the same. This intensifies. He confidently removes his T-shirt and I do the same. We shuffle to the bedroom, our lips still locked. Now I'm not going to describe what happened next. I'm keeping this between me and Ethan but I'm sure you get the picture.

We woke up together. He didn't look horrified by my bed head so he may in fact be a keeper.

'Good morning,' I say whilst smiling.

'Morning you. That was different.'

'That was hot.'

'Yeah it was good. Heck is that the time, I don't have long before work. I better go.'

'Oh sure, yeah do you want a shower or a coffee or something first?'

'I need to change my clothes, so I'll head back to mine and take a shower there.'

He scrambles to put his clothes on as he practically runs out the door. My perfect night followed by my imperfect morning. All day I'm glued to my phone. I stop myself from sending him a message. I don't know why? Not wanting to seem too keen or desperate, not understanding what is going on for him and pushing him away, trying to play it cool? By four o'clock I crack.

Jonathan – Hey hope you had a good day and that you were not late for work. Are you going to the gym later?

Ethan – Hi. Yes made it to work on time, just! I'm going to give myself a night off the gym, feeling tired so going to have a rest day. Have a good work out if you decide to go.

Jonathan – Yeah probably will. Thanks.

I go the gym. I feel like crap. Am I being ghosted? Am I being used? Now he's had his fun, he's moved on to the next guy? I don't think so, we would have slept together much sooner than a month of hanging out together if that was his intention. Maybe I wasn't good, or not what he was looking for? He's a Personal Trainer not an actor, he looked like he enjoyed himself. He came twice. Oh, wait I wasn't going to share those details. After my workout I start my usual tasks of walking Raff and then getting ready for bed. As a settle down for the night with my last cup of tea my phone pings.

Ethan – Hey hope your evening was okay. I feel I need to explain about rushing out this morning. I think I just scared myself a bit. I've not been with many guys before and when I have it has just been a one-night stand with a stranger. It was an amazing night which took me by surprise as no one knows I have feelings for men. I've kept those hidden, to others and myself, I guess. Sorry probably more complicated than you wanted.

Jonathan – Hi thanks for the message. Was trying to work out what was going on as I could sense something was up. We could just take things slow. No pressure here. I'm still trying to make sense of past relationships myself.

Ethan – Cool thanks for being so understanding. So, would you be up for meeting again like that?

Jonathan – Hell yeah!

Ethan – Great. Really enjoyed it. Been thinking about it all day.

Jonathan – Ha, me too.

Ethan – So heading to bed now as genuinely tired. See you tomorrow?

Jonathan – I'd like that.

Ethan – Great, night.

Jonathan – Night x

Ethan – x

I sip my tea with the biggest smile and feeling of warmth. Not from the earl grey but the thought of Ethan. I'm okay with just seeing what happens. My life has been trying to plan every detail of everything. I need to not overthink this and just let it be.

***

We continue to hang out, just as friends at places like the gym, and more than friends behind closed doors. Over the next few weeks, we speak daily, we pretty much see each other every day too. It's all very casual which I think I can handle. I have to stop myself obsessing over everything but it feels okay. Actually, it feels more than okay. I learn about his life, how he has, and still does I guess, struggle with his sexuality. To me it seems like a nonissue, I told my mum I was gay when I was about nineteen and although it was an initial shock she accepted it immediately. I remember saying to my mum, 'you're surprised, but I've never had a girlfriend.' My Dad I told in the pub and I think his reply was, 'that's cool.' In truth they knew before I did. For Ethan, it's a bit different. He talked about the expectations from his family and coming from a very male dominated work environment where he didn't think it was okay to like men.

After Adam, a friends with benefits arrangement suits me fine. Doesn't it? I am okay with this right? Yeah of course I am. I'm not having to waste time on social media, I've met someone who I like spending time with, and I don't need to stress about where it is going. Okay. Let's just go with it then.

Ethan takes me on a camping trip. This is my idea of hell but in the spirit of trying new adventures I go. My only other experiences of camping were going to V Festival with Tom when we were about twenty. The music was amazing but I hated camping. We were surrounded by all these chavs, the toilets were disgusting and I got no sleep at all. Oh, and I did an overnight in a tent with Adam once which again wasn't fun. 'This will be different, you'll love it.' I was assured. I didn't love it; communal wash rooms, a hard and cold bumpy ground, insects everywhere. Even Raff had an unsettled time. A bit too close to nature for us. I did love spending time with Ethan though. I'm starting to feel more natural around him, like I don't need to filter what I do and say. I like that.

We keep our usual Saturday night haunt of the cinema. I do like a good film and any excuse to go wild on the pick n mix. On one occasion as we are about to walk into the screen there is a shout from someone across the foyer. 'Ethan.' We turn around.

'Yo Ethan, How's it going man?'

'Hey what's up man?'

They shake hands but not in a conventional way, almost like the start of an arm wrestle in mid-air.

'All good, it's all good. You playing Sunday?' The guy who I'm yet to be introduced to so can't tell you his name asks.

Ethan replies, 'No man. My knee is still fucked up init. Not played for weeks.'

'Ah too bad man.'

'Hopefully I'll be playing soon before the end of the season.'

'Cool, well take care.'

I felt invisible. I wasn't expecting him to introduce me as, 'here's Jonathan my secret boyfriend' or 'the guy who had my cock in his throat last night,' but he could have said something. I felt a right lemon just standing there. I didn't say anything. Instead, we watched our film and then on the drive back my verbal diarrhoea exploded.

'So who was your mate?'

'Oh that was Rob, a football friend.'

'Yeah I figured out the football link.'

'Are you okay?'

'I was expecting you to introduce me. It felt like you were embarrassed by me.'

'Not at all. Sorry I didn't mean anything by it.'

I thought I was okay with the way things were. I think I was so focused on what Ethan needed, I neglected how I truly felt. It's taken forty years to become the person I am. I'm not prepared to hide any aspect of that.

'I'm sorry but I can't do this anymore. I thought I was okay but I'm not. I need more than this. I want someone to be with me for me. I can't be someone's secret lover.' Long pause. For god's sake say something, I think.

'I can't,' pause again, 'you know,' another pause (it feels the silences are saying more than Ethan) 'I'm not ready to be out.'

'Well you are not ready to be with me then.' There is an even longer silence as we have five minutes of the drive left before we get to mine. As he pulls up I say, 'do we have anything else to say?'

'You knew my history when we got together, I've never promised you anymore than this.'

'I know, and I thought I was okay with it, but I know now this is not enough.'

'So this is a good bye then?'

'I guess it is.'

I get out of the car and walk towards the front door. I'm tempted to look back, but I don't. In my flat I'm greeted by Raff who I hold and squeeze hard. I find myself single again.

Additional Chapter

I wasn't going to write this next chapter. I think it would be easier to try and forget rather than share, but in the spirit of transparency and this being a true picture of my fortieth year, here we go. Late one night and feeling low I reach for the crutch or portal for escapism which I have been using. I scroll through the list of whom now seem familiar faces. Little squares who all seem trapped in the app. A message pops up.

Fun – Evening, you ok?

Jonathan – I'm well thanks, how are you?

You'd think everyone is tired of these same conversations and would be using more imaginative ways of introducing oneself.

Fun – I'm horny.

Jonathan – Ha, who isn't? Getting a bit late tho.

Fun – You not looking for fun?

Jonathan – Not sure, what do you have in mind?

Fun – Anything really, I'm vers. Into the usual things. Could be fun.

Jonathan – Maybe.

Fun – You'll have to come to me. I'm a bit tipsy.

Jonathan – Okay that's cool.

Our chat continues in this nature, you get the picture by now, until I find myself parked up outside his house. I know I shouldn't judge like I do, but it was a bit of a rough area. Not one but two old, discarded washing machines greeted me at the front of his cul-de-sac. I proceed with caution and am greeted by a guy accurately described by his profile pictures; mid-forties, five foot nine, carrying a bit of weight but not fat, blonde hair in a slightly thinning and dated style. I could summarise as saying he was acceptable and a distraction from Ethan.

As he invites me into his house, I can see he is more than tipsy. He is drunk. I am impressed that he is able to write so articulately in his state. My first thought is wondering if he will be able to get it up. He goes to kiss me, and I taste a sweet flavour. I think it must be some kind of energy drink which he's been mixing with the half bottle of vodka I can see on the table behind. It's not unpleasant, just noticeable. 'Shall we go up to my bedroom?' he slurs.

'Yeah sure.' Although I'm not sure.

His bedroom is one that resembles that of a student bedroom rather than that of a man in his mid-forties. It's clean, ish, but very messy. CDs on the floor from where he had recently played them. I didn't realise people still play CDs. Another bottle of vodka, this time empty and multiple other objects scattered around the place, too many to mention here. The room is harshly lit which even, I'm going to call him David, recognises so he turns the light off leaving only the small crack of moon light shining through the curtains. I don't mind this though.

We kiss and move to the bed for stability. At least I think it's the bed, it looked more like a sofa with bedding on it. I think it might have been from Ikea, one of those day beds, I think they are called. Sorry, irrelevant detail. We continue to kiss and undress each other. I'm not enjoying myself and question at what point it would be acceptable for me to leave. He reaches for poppers which he sniffs and then offers them to me. I take them and then feel a bit more spirited. We kiss again and he caresses my body. I hear a clicking sound from outside. At first, I think it is his cat which I spotted earlier, then realise it was the bathroom pull cord.

'What's that noise? Are we not alone?'

'It will be my house mate, but he is going to bed now,' he slurs. I feel uncomfortable to the fact that there is someone the other side of the door who could be hearing everything. It reinforces this feeling of wanting to leave but I now feel if I do this now, his housemate will know he's had a disastrous meet, so I stay. I know, writing this now I think what messed up logic.

He smears lube on my arse and most of my leg due to his drunkenness as I lie there on my back with my legs raised. He pushes his dick into me whilst trying to kiss me. I however turn my face slightly. I didn't feel like kissing him. I don't want him inside me, but he continues to penetrate me. Again, writing this I can see the messed-up logic. I stop him from kissing me, but not fucking me? I think it was easier to turn my head rather than try and move him off me. He's hovering over me like a big lump, and I can feel the weight of his body. I lie still as he continues. I think and hope that he might just cum quickly and it will be over.

A few minutes in and I push his thighs away from me, but he ignores this.

'I should go,' I whisper in fear of his

housemate hearing.

'Not yet,' he replies.

'I only had time for a quick meet.'

'A bit more,' he says. As he does, he places his arms around my neck, he doesn't grip them as such, he actually places them quite delicately. He continues to thrust, and I continue to just lie there. I now think I've had enough. I push on his thighs again, which he ignores. I do so with more force which pushes him off the bed and he lands on the mess on the floor which makes a clatter.

'I do need to leave now,' I tell him quite forcefully.

'Okay,' he replies. I search for my clothes as he reaches for the light. The strong lighting suddenly comes on and when I see him again, he looks startled and red faced. I quickly get dressed, not caring that my T shirt is on inside out. As he looks for his manky dressing gown to put on, I reach for a bottle of Tom Ford aftershave which was on the floor and put it in my pocket. I felt like I needed to take something from him.

'Okay, bye,' I say to him as I kiss him on the lips. I know, why?

'Bye then,' he replies as he follows me out to the door.

The relief I feel as I walk to my car. I get in and I put the lock on, something I rarely do. I spray the aftershave and take a deep breath in, I feel comforted by that familiar smell. As I drive back, I try and process what went on and what just happened. I conclude that I allowed that car crash of a meet to happen and it was within my power to stop that earlier if I wanted to. I didn't though. It was the fear of upsetting him, or embarrassing him which I prioritised over me.

Chapter 26

Tom and Steve (and Carol)

I'm in a reflective mood and I'm thinking about Tom and Steve. They sound like a couple don't they, but they are as far removed as an item you could get. My two other significant relationships in my life. Polar opposites. If they were at a dinner party, I have no idea what they would talk about, however, I had, and still have a connection to them both.

I met Tom when I was twenty years old. He

was my first relationship. I had only been on two dates before that, and in truth, I don't really think I could really call either of those dates. This was before the days of Grindr but Gaydar. Whatever happened to that site? Oh wait, there was another guy who sort of befriended me and took me out on the gay scene. I don't remember his name now, maybe Paul? Anyway, there was a real innocence to my relationship with Tom, we lived in a little cocoon; just him and me. Both introverts, we didn't socialise with others. This was fine at the start but overtime I did feel that we were missing out on something.

Our time was spent always doing something; day trips, cinema, meals out. We ate out a lot. His family were adorable. I never had the relationship where I'd do anything with them on my own like take his mum to the garden centre or make coleslaw together at Christmas (or any other buffet item come to that), but I knew they loved me. Tom's sister has learning disabilities and continued to live at home into adulthood. As a result, his family stayed in that caring for a child mode and I think failed to see his sister, and Tom for that matter, as adults. He continued to get what can only be described as weekly pocket money and a great big bag of groceries every time he would visit, which was always twice weekly on a Wednesday and Saturday. I would sometimes go too but never regularly as I did not want to create a pattern where there was an expectation I would always be there.

His mum made the best Spaghetti Bolognese which is odd as she was a terrible cook other than this. She was always worried about giving anyone food poisoning so she would always cook meat for an extra half an hour no matter what size or cut, as a result it was always dry and like jerky. But so generous. I once made the mistake of saying I liked Toffee Crisps, for the next two years I had a pack of five every week. To this day I can't eat one as I've consumed so many. My other memory of Tom's mum was that she used a lot of tin foil. She's wasn't able to just tear a small amount to wrap something but would cover it ten times over, I don't know why she did this.

Like his mum, Tom was a very sweet man. Every morning and evening he would put the toothpaste on my brush and leave it on the side. That's just one of a number of small things he would do. I'm seeing this as an act of kindness, hopefully I didn't just have halitosis and he didn't feel able to tell me. It felt like it was him and me against the world. I think I'm still searching to replace this feeling. I thought I had it with Adam, but obviously not, and I'd started to feel it with Ethan. However, overtime Tom started to get quite cynical with life. Well, that's how I experienced it. I wonder if that's because he started to feel unhappy in our relationship? The truth is, the us when we got together at twenty, was different to the us fifteen years later. As people we started to change. That's fine I guess, that's inevitable, but the change pushed us apart rather than growing us together.

Overtime the intimacy went from our relationship, then the affection. What did this leave? Comfort. We were like Bert and Ernie. It was very comfortable being in Tom's company. He probably is, or was – five years on our relationship has changed again – the one person who I could be completely myself around. I could spontaneously dance or sing which I've not done with anyone else. I hope that's not lost forever.

We were together for fifteen years, we had a civil partnership, we laughed, we joked, we lived. It's fair to say what we didn't do was have wild passionate sex. Although at the time, because he was my first love, I didn't know any different so for a long time didn't question it. For a while I wondered if I was asexual. I know now I'm not. Or maybe I was then, and sexuality is fluid.

I look back on my time with Tom with fondness, I wouldn't change a thing. I had fifteen years of stability, and this helped me grow and become the person I am today. It also made me realise what I'm searching for. I want the equality and companionship that I had with Tom, with the passion and fun of Adam. I'm still trying to make sense of my feelings for Adam. When we met, he was in a transitional period in his life and unhappy. I think I tried to save him. That's why I have been struggling to move on because I still feel like his keeper. Even when in my head he was with Hank.

I was given a book end to my relationship with Tom. I had just come back from a Californian holiday with Steve (more about him in a bit) and on the Saturday I had returned went to pick up some glasses I had ordered. My optician's branch had closed down so they sent me to another one ten miles away. I took Raff and Steve's dog with me and as I was walking up the hill towards the optician's I could see two guys holding hands. At first they looked like Lego people in the distance but as they got closer I could see it was Tom and his new partner. I was pleased that I was looking all sun kissed but I was also pleased for him. Tom never held my hand. Or maybe I didn't hold his? I called his name but he didn't hear. I shouted, 'Tom,' but he still didn't hear. I don't think he was expecting to see me. I shout loud, 'TOM'.

He looked startled, his partner more so.

'Hello, how are you?'

'I'm good, just picking up some glasses.'

'Who's this?'

'Oh that's Rex.'

I hug Tom and then shake his partner's hand, I know, very formal. The small talk is minimal but

I walk away feeling like it was the perfect end to our relationship. It felt good to see that he had moved on.

***

Steve was my other significant relationship. We were together for nine months. He was fifteen years older than me, financially stable, confident, outgoing and I'm going to use the word head strong. He had a right way of doing everything and overtime I started to conform to this way. This started to worry me as I didn't know if my voice was starting to be diluted in conforming to what I thought he was looking for and the way things should be done. I'm talking minor things here, like the way to make a cup of tea. I'm always milk first, he was milk last. Squeezing the toothbrush from the bottom; does it really matter? Always ensuring no splash marks were left around the wooden worktop by the sink. It scared me that I was starting to be malleable to his life.

Don't get me wrong. It was a great life; road trips around California, flying first class, driving Porsches, meals out. We moved in together after just six months of meeting. I know, way too soon. When I was moving in, I knew in the back of my mind it was too soon, but I stayed ignorant to this and went along with the excitement of it all. Thankfully I didn't sell or completely rent my flat. I just let a room and I moved into the box room as

I still planned to stay there a couple of nights mid-week rather than deal with the longer commute to work. I hate traffic. I explained to my lodger that I'll hardly be there so effectively he'd have the full use of the flat. There was a time when I thought I could probably reduce my hours in work to part time and have this amazing life of living in a house in the country and driving around in fast cars. I then realised that I do want to drive a Porsche, but one that I brought and not had handed to me. It was only a few weeks after moving in that I was moving out. Only now I had a lodger that I didn't really want and I was residing in the box room!

In truth, I wasn't ready for a relationship with Steve. It was too soon after splitting with Tom, and then our time together was too soon in trying to be this established power couple with the dream lifestyle. In fact, Adam was too soon after Tom and I think some of the grieving this past year is for him too. I hope Steve's happy as he deserves this. I'm still good friends with him. After we split, which was a very hard thing to do, we still met up and occasionally fooled around, however this stopped both of us from moving on. Somehow beyond this we have managed to remain friends.

***

I've just realised that I lied to Carol. You know the Sexual Health Nurse? I have paid for sex, well sort of. This wasn't me trying to be deceitful or shameful of the fact, I genuinely completely forgot and it's just popped into my head. It was shortly after Tom and I split, and I was feeling down, I couldn't be bothered with scrolling through Grindr so when I was approached on the app by this one guy offering his services for £60 I took it.

'What's on offer?'

'Anything you want. You do need to pick me up though, I don't have a car and can't accommodate.'

After the odd exchange of photos which were semi-revealing I find myself parked outside his house waiting to take him back to mine.

As soon as he got into the car I could tell he was nervous. I quickly worked out he hadn't done this before. I didn't know his name but he was younger than me, say in his mid-twenties. He was a bit chavvy with grey trackie bottoms and a matching hoodie. As we made small talk to pass the time he told me that he was saving up money for his son's birthday present. I don't recall what he was buying him, a game console or something. I think he was genuine in telling me this.

Back at mine he followed me up the stairs to my flat and we went straight to my bedroom. I asked him if I should pay him now or afterwards and he wasn't sure.

'I'll pay you now,' I said as I took three crisp £20 notes from my wallet.

He was practically shaking with nerves as we go to kiss. Our lips barely touched and I stopped.

'You know what, we don't have to do anything if you don't want to,' I explain. 'Keep the money and I'll just take you back.'

He looks relieved. 'Are you sure?'

'Yes, honestly, it's fine. Here have this as well.' I handed him a further £50.

'Really, are you sure?'

'Yes, you buy that present.'

There was an instant change in his body language and he became more alive. He hugged me and it was genuine warmth.

'Thank you so much. What's your name?'

'Jonathan.'

'Thanks Jonathan.'

For the entire drive back he animatedly told me everything about his son. I pretended to be interested whereas in reality I didn't care. How he separated from his son's mother, how he sees him as often as he can and how he's going to be so thrilled to get his present. As we pull up to the same spot I literally was forty minutes ago we say our goodbyes.

'Thank you again,' he said and we exchange another hug. I smile. Driving home I have a good feeling, not quite the feeling of satisfaction I had planned but a good feeling all the same. I'm still not sure if I made a little boy's birthday the best it could be or supplied a week's worth of dope for his father, but either way I drive back feeling warm and fuzzy.

Chapter 27

Mexico

I decide I need some time to myself, I need a break from everything. This time, a proper holiday. Not one where I have to compromise by eating in a restaurant yet again because they serve pasta which is the only food my nieces eat. So that's what I do, on my own. The planning part of a holiday I absolutely love. My OCD, which I try and keep hidden, has an outlet. When Tom and I once went to New York for our honeymoon, many moons ago, we planned every hour of that trip within an inch of its life. We spent days putting together a detailed itinerary for every thirty minutes of the five days we were there, I loved it. I think I still have the Excel spreadsheet. The holiday was great too, but I loved the planning aspect. It's a chance for my organisational skills to shine. After much research I opt for a beach holiday in Mexico.

I am a bit worried how I'm going to cope. I'm one of these people who will be walking along the high street and pop into a shop and come out and walk back in the wrong direction. I do it literally every time. My sense of direction is just rubbish. I also get lyrics to songs completely wrong. I always thought 'Red light, smells danger' and in the Bee Gees' You Win Again was actually 'you alligator'. I know, my lyrics are better. I'm not sure why I shared that as it's not all that relevant. Face slap.

***

It's a silly o'clock flight so I decide to stay in a hotel near to the airport the night before. It's a Saturday night, about seven o'clock and I'm hungry. I've never been to a restaurant on my own before, well maybe McDonalds but I'm not sure if that really counts. I'm going to be eating on my own each night, well unless I find some handsome Mexican to feed me enchiladas, so I think I might as well try it out now.

Walking along the high street for eateries I realise I'm treading couples' territory. Already I feel alone and small. What confidence I have shivers into itself and I walk with trepidation. Literally every restaurant is filled with tables for two with these hot couples looking affectionately into each other's eyes. I feel intimidated to go in and think I'll settle for a takeaway pizza back in my hotel room. Wait, I spot this hot guy in the window of the restaurant on his own. He's super fit with a tight fitted muscle tee showing off his arms and tan. He's eating alone, so I could do that too. I have visions of us being seated next to each other. I casually drop a spoon and we both reach down to pick it up at the same time. Maybe our heads lightly collide, we lock eyes and smile as we then go on to chat for the entire evening. Now someone really needs to tell me that I don't live in a Disney movie. I can live in hope. Right, I'm going in, I'm going to do this.

'Hi, do you have a table, I've not booked?'

'Let me see, how many of you will be dining this evening?'

Why ask this question, it's obvious I'm alone? 'Just me, a table for one please,' I say quite proudly.

'Follow me,' I'm told in quite an abrupt fashion. Why are maître d's so bossy? We walk towards hot guy and I start to get excited. This could be it. I take the seat so I'm opposite him, albeit at a different table, for now anyway. I'm sure we'll get the waiter to merge our tables at some point.

Just as I look up, he looks over at me and gives the biggest smile. I can feel myself blushing, what to do? I'm going to have to smile back. As I give my biggest smile revealing my big pearly white teeth, I realise he was not in fact smiling at me, but his girlfriend who had just returned from the bathroom. Now my view is of a bleach blonde with big hair who smells like a perfumery. My entire evening is spent sitting awkwardly eavesdropping on their conversation. I know I didn't have to listen but there wasn't much more I could do and you know my love of people watching. Whilst sitting in the restaurant I had the same feeling I had whilst waiting to be picked for the football team at school. Lanky Jonathan with his big fluffy hair not helped by my undercut which gave even more volume as I walked. I was always second from last to be picked. David Dawson being last, he was more camp than me. I'm digressing but it was a similar inadequate, come unwanted, come inferior, feeling. God they're dry. In fact, I've probably saved myself there.

I promptly ask for the bill as soon as I finish my first and only course and quickly down my pint of larger so I can leave at the earliest possible moment. I don't think I can take another story from hot guy and bleach blonde whilst they chat about reality television. Back in my hotel room I decide to ring my mum before my very early alarm call for a five o'clock flight.

'You got there safe? Have you packed everything? Do you have a universal charger? Are you nervous? Are you going to be ok?'

'Yes, yes, yes, no, yes.'

Then wait for it, 'you take care my love, give me a ring when you get there, I love you'.

I smile, 'I love you too mum.'

The next day I'm awoken by my alarm and I excitedly get my belongings together and head to the airport. I manage to navigate myself through check-in and make it to the airport lounge where I wait patiently for my flight to be called. Aren't airports such an amazing place? They never sleep. Tom and I used to go to the airport to have a Burger King. It was like a kind of date night. Before the term date night came into existence that is.

You can't do that now with all the security but twenty years ago you could. It's such a great place for a people watcher like me. On cue I'm trying to pass myself off as that cosmopolitan, international traveller. I think I manage it with a tight-fitting white shirt buttoned down to more than I usually would and tight-fitting beige chinos with some brogues which I later regret on the flight when me feet get hot and sweaty. For now though, I look just the part.

Flight Number MEX1224 to Mexico is now boarding at Gate 33. Exciting this is it. Sun, sea and no sex is calling me. I'm under no illusions that I'm going to meet anyone on this holiday, this is my way of just relaxing and escaping the memories of Adam and Ethan. Adam and Ethan, sounds like the gay Adam and Eve. More waiting prevails as we wait to board the flight. There really is a lot of waiting around at an airport isn't there? I'm not that good at it, I'm far too impatient but wait we will. Then we get to board, and we are off. It's a long uneventful flight, although I do achieve a personal best on Solitaire, still a very average score I expect but it passed the hours away. Then as we get to leave, and I step off the plane I'm greeted by that amazing warmth again. I love that sensation.

Checking into the hotel I'm very conscious that I'm alone amongst many other couples and families. I'm so proud of myself for doing this but it is a bit daunting. I'm out of my comfort zone at a time when I'm seeking a holiday to relax so there is some kind of paradox to this. Of course, I'm not the only singleton here. There's the lovely cat lady who equally is trying to relax but constantly checking up on how her nine babies are coping without here. I hear her on the phone. 'Remember Tily is lactose intolerant, and Amber needs a grain free diet for her digestion, and they all need to sleep on a goose feather pillow not synthetic,' Heck, is this what I'll become one day? Instead of cats I'll be this crazy dog man with dogs in the double figures and I'll call them my fur babies. I miss Raff now, I'm sure he'll be fine without me. Apart from the month of Ethan and my week away with the family it has just been him and me these past eight months so he is probably appreciative of the break.

Immediately after checking into my room I hit the pool, and this is where I stay pretty much for the whole holiday. It is bliss. As with a new relationship there are lots of firsts, so too when holidaying alone. My first venture to the restaurant, alone. Why do they sit you at the worse table possible? I might be on my own but I still want to be part of what's going on. They may have well just given me a toilet cubicle I was so close to them! Although the advantage was that I was able to people watch to pass away the time.

I'm not a reader so whereas I've seen other single holiday makers take a book to read with them whilst they eat, this feels alien to me. I look at my phone a lot. I've never been one for Facebook or Instagram but I do find myself on there much more than normal. I guess I'm trying to connect to people. It's scary how big the world is, and I'm on the other side of it on my own. I feel small right now. I find it more bizarre that the world is just part of our solar system which in turn is part of the universe. We really are a tiny, tiny,

tiny, tiny (I could keep on going) dot. Yet we often give such high status and importance to what we do. Whereas would it really matter if I was not around? Family and friends will be sad, but I'm sure they'll get over it. Someone else will need to feed and walk Raff.

I do have another first, my first book I read from cover to cover in about twenty years. It was Maurice by E. M Forster. Recommended by my friend Fliss. She's very well read. I know what you are thinking, a bit highbrow for someone who is writing this dribble. I loved it, it's such a beautiful love story. I felt sad at the end even though it was a happy ending. I'm not sure why I felt this, maybe I was longing for my Alec or just a happy ending, which I feel so far removed from at the moment. The book was not published until after the author's death. He never will know the impact that book had on others.

I learn that the problem with holidaying alone, is that other single holiday makers are drawn to you. Most people there were Americans and only a few Brits. There was one guy, Ricky Grant, who really latched onto me, and it was so hard to shake him off! Bloody Ricky Grant, he popped up everywhere. A gay man in his early 50s, he looked like a character from the League of Gentleman, he spoke so loudly and loved telling everyone who just glanced at him that we had struck up a friendship and that I had just been dumped by my boyfriend weeks before. He had no filter, at all. No awareness that I wanted to be left alone. We dined together once, he asked if he could join me and I didn't have the heart to say no, then he tried to do that every evening. In the end I had to make up pretend excursions then hide or spend the whole day at the other end of a scorching beach in disguise with my hat and glasses.

I heard his WHOLE life story. How our Lyndsey is going through a divorce again, she's the one who married her first husband at eighteen and didn't tell the family, then she got pregnant, and the father got arrested and sent to prison. Then when he got out he found out she was pregnant again to his best mate Trevor and they had to flee to Newcastle as they were worried about what he'd do to them. I learnt about his mum and her varicose veins. There was also Billy, he works with him at the Pie factory, he's twenty years younger but fancies Ricky and once gave him a blow job in the boss's office when they were left to lock up. Oh, and his Aunty Catherine who had a Botox injection which went wrong and she had a crooked smile for four months. I've got about a million more of these stories all scarred to memory. My worse memory though was when his shorts fell down whilst getting out of the pool to reveal his hairy butt and I can share with you that his mother's health issues run in the family.

In addition to hiding from Ricky, I did manage to have a good time and eventually found my voice to tell him to piss off. Well, maybe I was not that direct. I wasn't direct at all. I told him Ethan and I were back together and he would be jealous if he knew I was chatting to another man. Ricky swallowed this and gave his attention to the bar man, who he did break our pact to tell me he got sucked off by for a shot of Tequila. My shot for yours, the story went, apparently. Eww, I need a shower.

There was one holiday romance, I couldn't help but see who was on Grindr and came across this beefy, good-looking guy and arranged a meet. I didn't realise though the hotels in Mexico are guarded and he got challenged for not being a guest. I had to pay £100 for him to get a visitors pass for the day but heck it was worth every penny of it. We ended up having dinner afterwards and it was nice to see the waiting staff not feeling sorry for me for either dining alone or dining with the chatty man.

He was called Sergio. Ha, I've just realised my reality is starting to become my imagination of Adam's life back when we first broke up. I don't think I could have seen it then. There is movement for me. Anyway, he was half Mexican and half American. He had the fattest dick. I wasn't expecting it as from the pictures he sent it was in proportion to his chunky thighs. It was a very good night, not rushed like most Grindr meets. Maybe I was conscious to try and get my money's worth. He was a great kisser and someone who I felt appreciated me and my body. We said we would keep in touch and friended each other on Facebook but the contact soon dried up.

My holiday was bliss. Yoga on the beach, running bare foot on the sand when my lungs could allow it, I'm still smoking. For me a holiday is just doing absolutely nothing. I had the chance to do an excursion to the Temple of Kukulcan, one of the seven wonders of the world, which I passed up to just roast myself on the beach. My sister was horrified I didn't take this opportunity but I love just doing nothing, listening to music and reflecting on my thoughts. Thank you Mexico and thank you Sergio, you helped me.

Chapter 28

Craig

Ok it's smut time again. Sorry all. This is me embracing my single life though. I think I'm making up for time in my youth. I was too much of a prude to do anything risky or sexual when I was younger. Then I met Tom and we were together for fifteen years. I'm care free and young again. Well, with the exception of my grey hair already poking through and my achy legs. I have no idea why they are aching. Anyway, what can I tell you about Craig? There is the Craig I met on our couple of sexual encounters, then there is the Craig whom I have come to love and hold with the deepest regard and affection. Let's start with the first one though.

One Sunday morning Craig arrives at my flat. We have been messaging for a while trying to arrange a meet but something had always gotten in the way so it has never came to fruition. However, this Sunday it happens and he arrives with a great big bag. Is he moving in? I think to myself. No, he's just come with multiple outfits he later gets me to wear and model for him. All shiny lycra pieces of skimpy pants, and well, I don't know what it was. I've been looking online for the name but it's like a wrestling costume. He has loads of them alongside other toys and goodies we try out.

Let me set the scene first and describe Craig. I found him more attractive in person than his photos. My reasons for wanting to meet him were less about sexual attraction, but more because of his interests which I was looking to explore. He was very much into nipple play, tick, a hairy manly top with an array of kinks. He had short black hair with piercing blue eyes, a combination I'd not seen since Ethan. Oh Ethan... wrong timings again there. Sigh.

Now as you can tell, I'm starting to enjoy sex. I guess I always have and see it as a healthy part of my life. Although interestingly, the more I have, the more I want. When I went through a dry spell a few months ago, after a while I didn't miss it, or long for it, I think I even gave up wanking after a while. However, when I jumped back on the horse, so to speak, my sexual drive ignited. For me though, sex has always just been a quick thirty-minute rumble, and I'm satisfied. Then I'd move onto the next thing, which inevitably involved food. Craig saw sex as a working day. Longer, in fact, with the time going into double figures. That was one of the reasons I didn't see him as boyfriend material, I'd just be shattered all the time. That and as I started to learn more about him, I started to see him as a friend and learned that his heart was much bigger than his overstretched nips, strangely I became less interested in him sexually but what developed was a friendship.

Within our exchange of texts, before we met, he boasted how he likes to come several times. This wasn't uncommon based on the other message encounters I had with guys, but in reality, once a guy comes he's no longer interested in sex again. Craig was different. He was obsessed with wanting to ejaculate multiple times. By the third time only a dribble came out but he was still obsessed with wanting to come again. In between his ejaculations I learned more about his life and the many sexual experiences he had had.

He first had sex at fourteen. He explained that he saw a telephone number in a toilet cubicle and rang it from his parents' house. The next day he bunked off school to travel up to London to meet this guy. In his words the guy was 'obese and covered in warts' but he loved it. He went the next week with a school friend, and then again the following week. His childhood years were spent cottaging in the local council toilets. 'Even now I get turned on by the sound of the hand dryers or the smell of those urinal squares,' he joked, 'it takes me back to my childhood.'

At seventeen he moved to Sydney and worked in a sex shop doing peep shows and glory holes. Again, these are fond years for him. Craig is only ten years my senior, but it feels like he has lived compared to me. My life is so boring. I grew up in sleepy Cornwall where I stayed until I was eighteen. University, boyfriend, job, house. I've travelled, but I've not really travelled. It's been all package holidays and hotel stays. Although to be fair that's what I like. I couldn't slum it anywhere.

Craig has been in a porno movie. I've never been in one of those. However, I don't think I would want to. Also, to be fair in my comparison, Craig's scene was cut for 'overacting.' He was dressed as a vicar and walked in on two guys having sex, like you do, and was told to just watch. Instead of watching he started to masturbate and gave his best 'oooh errrr' noises. I think his presence detracted from the main scene.

I later learn though that when he first met me, he felt intimidated by me. He thought I had everything; nice home, good job, good car, good teeth, maybe not so good hair. I think he would be shocked to hear how I see his worldliness in the way that I do. I wonder if that is a common thing where many see others as more successful than themselves. Anyway, I'm doing a bad job at describing my sex with Craig. How do I summarise?

Ten hour session
Nine times
Eight inches
Seven outfit changes
Six ejaculations
Five fag breaks
Four worked nipples
Three fingers
Two burgers and chips
One hole

We probably met twice after that for sex, then like I say, the sexual chemistry dissolved, and I was left with a great friend. Although how many friends can you say have waxed your arsehole? He's a professional waxer and one afternoon literally stripped every follicle of hair off my body. I was like ET at the end, well maybe less wrinkly. I hope. Sorry I've just read this chapter back. Overshare Jonathan.

He's also given me one of the biggest belly laughs I've had in my life. I think I nearly wet myself as he told the story. He recounted a time when he met a guy online who was from Amsterdam, I think it was, somewhere like that anyway. The guy paid for his travel and accommodation on the condition that he would fracture his leg in order to put it in a cast and then wheel him around for the trip. I know! Craig actually went. Once there he changed his mind regarding his leg being broken (sensible move) but agreed to being put in an upper body cast and where he was still wheeled around and attended a dinner party. I have visions now that make me laugh just imagining him being fed soup dripping down his cast. Craig admitted that he didn't really know what he got out of it, 'it was just something to do.'

He is a true friend and one of the most generous people I know. For his fiftieth birthday he paid for twenty of his friends to travel up to London to watch Cirque du Soleil. The only problem was the drinks were flowing so much I ended up having a bit too much and fell asleep throughout the entire performance. Then as I woke, or was awakened by an annoyed looking Craig. I had the urge to be sick, which is not good in a crowd of two thousand people. I found myself projectile vomiting in this corridor side bin of the Royal Albert Hall. Then, once outside, I found my complimentary programme tote bag very useful.

Not my finest moment. However, it's moment like which I realise I've been missing out on most of my life. I see this is what's important.

C h a p t e r   2 9

Distractions

I start my morning scrolling through Instagram liking various posts in the hope they will replicate the favour and either like or follow me. I know #pathetic. I need to expand my hobbies beyond dating and social media. Dating is good but it's still within a culture which feels quite alien, and as it starts to become more everyday, the acceptance of this is saddening. It's also very fake. It's very disposable. There is an investment that you need to give at the start of a conversation, and this becomes tiresome after a while. The same conversations and half of these go nowhere. How is it acceptable to just be ignored or ghosted midway through a chat? I need more in my life than this.

I've never really had any hobbies other than the gym and yoga. I decide to try my hand at golf. My Dad is an avid golfer. When I was about ten, for Christmas he brought me a set of golf clubs and all the attire that goes with it including junior membership to his club. I don't remember a lot about it, I doubt I was any good. My sister was good, she could whack the ball and could have gone pro apparently. My only memory was playing in a competition with these two old ladies. I think they felt sorry for me struggling to carry the heavy clubs and halfway through summoned one of their husbands to lend me the golf trolley. I've never been that sporty, but is golf really a sport? My Dad enjoys it as he's able to smoke. Now surely if you can smoke whilst doing it, it can't be a sport?

I arrive at the driving range with a collection of clubs in tow. The people there were polar opposites. One group of golfers are who you would expect to see; middle aged men who appeared wealthy. You could tell by the Jags and Mercedes in the car park. The other clientele was, well quite chavvy. They were a fairly young crowd of fit buff men. I felt quite intimidated by both groups and couldn't see myself fitting in. A bucket of 250 balls and a lane, or whatever the proper name for it is, as far away as possible from anyone else and I'm away. The only problem was it became busy so slowly I got absorbed within the crowds.

You would think it is easy. You just swing and the ball goes straight in the air. I remember what my dad used to say to me aged ten to try and help a smooth swing, as you swing back you say the word Sev-er-i-ano, and as I swing forward I say Ball-est-er-os. My dad loved that man. It wasn't enough for me though as I fail to even lift it from the air. It was so embarrassing, they were so close to the lane even that little hoover thing that picks them up didn't detect them. The rare occasion I do lift the ball from the ground I completely club it (think that's the term) and it hits the side and projects into the bay, bay that's what they are called, it hits the bay and nearly takes out Tarquin.

The only part I do enjoy is having a hot chocolate from the vending machine in the little thin plastic cup that comes with one of those holders. That took me right back to my youth where my sister and I would watch my dad hitting the balls into the night. We would name the flag for him to hit as we watched with our small drinking chocolate. Happy days, but days in the past and not part of my future I discover.

The next week I try something different.

235

Something which is more to do with who I am now. I decide to try Pole dancing. The instructor is amazing with her long pink hair, she's effortlessly cool. I wish I was an expert in something. I, however, very quickly realise that it's not going to be Pole dancing. It's silly as dancing is in the title but I didn't realise how coordinated and choreographed the steps in between getting up and down the pole actually are. Several times I land in a heap on the floor and think there is no way I can make this look elegant or sexy. I realise this is not for me and I need to find another hobby. I'm so glad I went though and was surprised at my confidence in trying this and not being nervous as I found the studio.

I've still got a sewing machine which I brought a few years ago but never used it because I couldn't get past my bobbins. I have this fantasy of someone complimenting me on an outfit and asking where I brought it, to which I reply, 'Oh I made this.' Perhaps I could dust that off.

The following week I try a different activity – step forward the Gay City Bowlers. I wasn't sure at first. Based on their Instagram page it looked quite competitive and that they took it pretty seriously. In preparation I offered to take my nieces bowling. Bless my sister she thought I was being a kind and thoughtful uncle whereas I was really going for my selfish gain. Yes my ten year old niece did beat me, and that was with the barriers up but I felt more confident to play with the bigger boys.

Turning up at the venue I was surprised by the number of guys there, over fifty I think. I was expecting a small handful. It was as if the Grindr grid had come to life and they jumped out of the screens in front of me. Thankfully no one I'd slept. Phew. What followed was such a fun night. No pretence, no showing off, no attempts to hook up, a few sexual innuendos involving large balls but that was to be expected I guess. I was absolutely rubbish but had such a good time. Sometimes I find, and this is where Judgy Jonathan is showing himself again, there is a particular type who might attend an organized event, but these people seemed normal. I was normal amongst them.

Back home I'm greeted by the ever so excited Raff. I love the fact he is always excited to see me. I could have just murdered a little old lady and he wouldn't care, he would still greet me with those big brown eyes and wagging tail whilst I wipe the blood from my arms and sleeve. There is always that undevoted affection. I wonder if that's what I want in a relationship. Maybe it will get tiresome after a while. Do I really want someone who will challenge me? My relationship with Tom during the first ten years or so felt like he put me on a pedestal. He would celebrate my half birthday as well as my actual one. That's just one example, I've forgotten others. That felt good but also felt like an imbalance at times as he only had one birthday every year. Do I even want a relationship at all, why are large chunks of society so fixated on being a couple? I mean, there's a massive industry around it, and this notion of finding your perfect soul mate. Does that really exist?

My next attempt to make myself interesting is bouldering. It looked easier than climbing but just as impressive on my profile. I think I should be good at this but get overtaken by the six year old girl. Yes as humiliating as starting on the children's wall is at least this is where I think I'll be better than everyone, I'm not. There's just no grip on my little hands. You would have thought I would be better from all the masturbating I'm doing in the absence of sex. My right arm is strong but my left lets me down. It's a good attempt though and I enjoyed chatting to the fit instructor with the long chest hair which couldn't be contained in his t-shirt. The same right hand enjoyed him later that evening.

That just reminds me. Has anyone else masterbated using Deep Heat? I had a shoulder injury the other day and just seeing it sitting there on my bedside table as I was pleasuring myself. As you can see I'm getting quite creative in my single life. Interesting sensation. Heck and I'm judging those who partake in organized events!

***

Adam emailed me today. He told me he was in Cornwall. He woke up one morning and felt he needed to be close to me. Clearly, he is struggling too. I wonder if all this time he's sitting there tapping away at a computer like me reflecting on what we had? His email came at the exact moment when I was thinking about him (yes, I still do), but what am I meant to do with that? I'm in a paradox in wanting to get back together but knowing this would not be right for him or me. I'm sticking with being alone though.

We exchange pleasantries about his wild swimming in the sea and the pasty he brought from our favourite bakery and various other messages in this vein. The last one from him ended in him telling me that he loved me. Head fuck. I decide I can't reply back saying that I don't feel the same way so I suggest I visit him instead. I know, probably not the smartest of moves but an hour later I'm buzzing on his front door. I don't really know what I'm feeling at this point. With situations like this, or a job interview or a first date or public speaking, I have this naïve courage where I don't think or worry about what might happen, but just do it. I can't work out if it's a good thing or not.

He answers the door wearing his gym kit and football socks which go up to his knees. His face looks worn. He's lost weight but is still super fit. A bit too muscular if that's a thing. His body fat must be really low and his veins are prominent. After the initial flutter of butterflies that jump from my heart, I think what a strange thing to wear and my first thought is that he's found a fetish in sports gear. I picture him with Hank who's wearing lycra. We hug and the embrace feels different. It feels like hugging a sparrow. Not that I've done that. Stay on track. I miss him but now there are questions in my head, which are already bubbling away. We chat and I can feel my protective barrier around me. I feel myself perching rather than sitting on his couch. He has a couch now. Before his flat was sparsely furnished which I don't think helped me feel comfortable being there.

He tells me that he's found it hard to move on, that he can't sleep in our bed and uses the spare bedroom, that every night he tells me that he loves me and kisses the headboard. I hear the words but question the sincerity which he immediately picks up on and accuses me of not being present. He's right, I guess. The gorgeous late Nanny Marion (known for her roasties - she part boiled them, drained the water and then fluffed them in a pan before roasting them with a very generous sprinkle of salt) used to kiss my grandfather's pillow after he died every night and told him that she loved and missed him. They were together for sixty years before his death and only slept apart a handful of nights when he went into hospital. I remember telling Adam this and he was moved to the point of tears. Is this why he's telling me about kissing the bed?

We do chat and joke more freely at times. His flat looks like a jungle with house plants. I spot the spider baby I once gave to him which is only recognisable from the pot. It has grown and blossomed in contrast to us. There's a smell of incense and I can see that he's making choices on how he wants his life to be.

I realise nothing has changed. Well his flat has changed. He's a bit more hippy like now. We havn't changed. If I was only seventy percent nine months ago, how am I what he is looking for now? I tell him this. I have a real sense that he needs to experience being on his own more, that he needs to experience being in other relationships to work out who he is and what he wants. I would just be a distraction from this.

This is true, I did mean these words and believe it is what he needs. Being truthful, this is what I need too. I don't want a relationship with him. What the fuck was the last nine months really about? Why didn't I realise this then? Why didn't I realise this three years ago when he first kissed me?

There were times when it would have been so easy to kiss him, but I stopped myself. It's not that I didn't want to. Part of me very much did, I just knew it would have been a mistake for both of us. That we both had more healing and growing to do before coming close to thinking we can either start afresh or build on what we had before. I leave and my drive back is full of brain fog. I realise there is movement for me. I feel empowered by this.

Chapter 30

Alex

It's time for another first date. Although they don't seem a firsts anymore. Quadruple date. This time it's Alex, a forty-seven-year-old single man who can only be described as going through a period of change in his life. He's currently off work due to sickness, which I learn on our walk is work related stress where he found himself screaming at his manager which apparently could be heard five offices away.

'I don't know what came over me, I just lost complete control. I've never done that before and it was so scary how I had no control over what I was doing.'

I can believe that from meeting him. He reminded me a lot of myself. He was a very reflective man, very self-aware, intelligent (heck I must also think a lot of myself) and funny. I think most people who are funny are clever too. You have to be in order to be quick witted.

We nearly didn't meet. A trend. He was going to drive to mine and then we were going to go for a walk with Raff but messaged me an hour before saying he couldn't drive because he had a bad back and had just picked up his car from the garage and just driving five minutes was agony. When I got that message, I initially thought it was an excuse. I'm getting used to that. We ended up with me travelling to a park near to him and I could see he had a genuine back pain. I've had back pain, I could sympathise, it's horrible.

We walk around and because we are so alike, the conversation is not high energy, but is still free flowing and I feel I've met my match in understanding my quirky humour. Alex is about my height, perhaps slightly taller. He has a big, fairly well managed beard, and he's bald, from shaving his head, not naturally. He looks a real man's man. I learn he used to play Rugby. He's wearing jeans and a shirt which reveals a good rug of hair on his chest. We stop and sit on the grass as we exchange Grindr stories.

'I swear, if everyone had a wank first before going online then I'm sure people would be less aggressive, and it would be a nicer place. But if they did this, then they probably wouldn't go online in the first place, so it's catch 22.'

He laughed and agreed. 'You know what, I think you are absolutely right there.'

He tells me about his two other recent dates. 'One guy was so touchy feeling it was unreal. He kept touching my arm and trying to stroke me'.

'On a first date?'

'Yes, he just wouldn't take no for an answer and kept trying to direct us to his flat even though I had already explained I wasn't looking for that. I think I could have buggered him there in the park if I wanted to!'

He explained his other encounter accused him of having pictures that didn't reflect him. 'I think they are pretty accurate.'

'Yeah me too.'

'Well he ended our date quickly by just saying I think we are done now, don't you?'

'Sounds like a bit of a prick.'

I feel very at ease talking to him and he gets points for being absolutely smitten by Raff. 'I want a dog but I can't have one because of my building lease.'

'Oh that's in my lease too but everyone just ignores it.'

'Not in mine they don't, you can't have any animals. My neighbour had a fish and when the management company found out they made him get rid of it. He had to flush the poor thing down the toilet!'

'Bet the AGM meetings must be great fun.'

'Ha, yes.'

We move onto relationships.

'So how long have you been single for?'

'Oh I... I'm... I... how do I say it?'

'You're not looking for a long-term relationship?'

'No, not that, I can't talk about it?'

There is a sadness as he says this. I think his ex must be either a real bastard or has died. I don't push the conversation and we just carry on talking about Raff and other things. I can see his back is hurting him, he's lying down on the grass and then occasionally gets up on his knees revealing his strong thighs and broad chest. There is something quite primitive in how he moves because of his back, and I find that a turn on.

We continue chatting and walking and I realise it's been about two hours. I still haven't learnt all that much about him, but I like what I see and hear. We say our goodbyes with a hug and belly rub, that was for Raff not me, although I wouldn't have said no to a belly rub from him.

Back home I leave it a few hours before messaging him. Well, I don't want to be seen as too keen.

Jonathan – Hey Alex… Good to meet you earlier… it's reassuring to know that there are normal/decent people out there. Hope your back clears up soon, Jonathan and Raff x

Alex – Hey Jonathan, A pleasure man. You're both good souls

Jonathan – I'll take that.

Alex – And your dog obviously loves me, btw.

Jonathan – Don't read too much into that… he's a bit of a slut when it comes to cuddles.

Alex – Aren't we all.

Alex – But nah. It was love.

Sadly, I don't hear from him again, but it just goes like that. I'm not going to over analyse it. This is the start of a new 'I'll go with the flow' easy going me.

Chapter 31

Friends

It was an unusual encounter for a friendship. In-between my time spent with Ethan and well just me, I had a meet with Matt, a guy in his mid-forties, or at least that's what he said, black, tall and sporty looking. I'm not sure what happened but somewhere between Matt sending the photos of him and my drive to his house, he lost his two front teeth and gained significant weight. That said, I had travelled thirty minutes and was feeling horny so found myself, well I no longer need to describe these things to you now. You get the picture. 'I can't stay long but would be up for some oral fun if you are up for that?'

'Well get on your knees then.'

As I was doing this, his phoned pinged.

'We might be joined by someone, if that's okay? He probably won't be round until about 1am.' 'Oh I'm definitely going to be gone by then,' I explained.

Another ping. 'He's in his Uber so will now be ten minutes.'

'Oh well I can go now in that case. Unless, have you got a photo?'

Matt shared a photo of an incredibly fit guy.

'He's my mate, he's one of those Nemos.'

'A Nemo?'

'Yeah he's a bit grungy and dresses in black.'

I should say at this point, Matt is either intoxicated or taken drugs. Evident from his flat and persona, I think he lives quite a chaotic lifestyle. I looked past this as I thought I won't be there long and won't be doing that much with him. Now, however, I see this Emo, or Nemo as Matt calls him, who, in actual fact, is not an Emo at all, I think I might stay longer.

'Will he be okay with me being here?'

'Yeah he's well up for it.'

'Okay, well maybe I could stay for a little longer.' This night is looking up.

There is a knock at the door and it's Jacques. He's French, which I'm sure you guessed by the name, thirty-three, tall, slim athletic and incredibly handsome.

'Hi, I'm Jonathan.'

'I'm Jacques' he said as he looked at me surprised to see me in the room pretty much naked apart from wearing a jock. He looked perplexed. He still removed his top to reveal a swimmer's body and amazing tattoo of a phoenix.

'So I can go, or I'm happy to stay for a bit.' I explain.

'Okay', he says in a super sexy accent. I realise something is wrong.

'Did you know I was going to be here?'

'No' he replies.

Matt interjects, 'ahh it's cool though.'

'So you two know each other, right?' I ask.

Matt replies yes, Jacques replies no, simultaneously. 'We've not met before'.

Matt now looks puzzled, 'I thought we had.'

'No I am pretty sure we haven't,' Jacques then asks for water.

'Sure, follow me into the kitchen, through here, you come too.'

We both follow, I'm still just dressed in my jock and Matt shows Jacques the bathroom for some reason and random objects around the home.

'I'm just after water if you have it.'

By this point we see the mess of his flat. 'I

haven't washed up in two weeks,' he says as he proudly refers to the stack of glasses on the kitchen side. 'I'm going to throw them out and just buy new,' he announces. As he does, he picks up a glass and gives it a rinse under the cold tap before handing it to Jacques. I think he's brave for taking it and then think to myself that I'd had Matt's cock in my mouth so actually which is worse?

Matt leaves the room with the expectation that we will follow.

'Are you okay?' I whisper.

'I don't think I can do this.'

'So you are not friends with him then? He was making out like you were close.'

'No, I've messaged him but we've never met. Where I have deleted profiles, I can't remember the full extent of our conversations but we have never met. He is not like his photo and this place is a mess.'

'Yeah, it was a bit spontaneous for me, and when I got here, I thought what the hell but that I won't stay long. Then when he said you were coming, I thought I would stay because, well you're fit, but if you are not staying then I might go too.'

I felt an instant connection to him. He had an endearing feature to him.

'I'm not going to stay. He is off his face on drugs and not making any sense.'

I, perhaps selfishly, inform Matt first that I'm going to leave.

'Yeah that's cool man.'

As I dress there is an awkward silence as Jacques scrambles for words. I feel like a fly on the wall.

'I am sorry, this is not working for me and I am going to leave too.'

Matt looks disappointed.

'You are going to leave … Yeah man, that's cool, it's fine if you want to stay or if you want to go.'

Jacques can't find his top and there is a moment where I could see him thinking he might just leave without it rather than prolong the awkwardness. I then find it on the floor. We say our goodbyes to Matt before promptly leaving.

'Do you want a lift? My car is right there,' I say pointing to it.

'If you don't mind.' As I drive Jacques back to his flat, with the initial intention to play, I realise that I think I like him more as a friend than a conquest. He invites me up for coffee as we continue to unpick what just happened, and talk more widely about life, past relationships, work and other interests. We talk for two hours as he sips peppermint tea and I have strong black coffee.

There were two things in his flat that stood out for me. On his cupboard door was a post it with the words 'you are good enough' written on it. The other were red high heel shoes which I later learn he has a desire to dance in but doesn't have the confidence to try. It's through moments like these do I realise connection with people is really what I'm missing. 'I'd better go, I have my dog to get back for. Let's swap numbers though, will be good to keep in touch. Perhaps a dog walk at the weekend?'

'I would really like that.'

There was a sense of Jacques feeling lost. He had just moved to the city for work. We bonded over being gay, single and making sense of life, in addition to the surreal evening we both shared.

I realise I am a people person. I didn't see that the significant thing missing in my life were friends, but through dating and chatting to guys online I realise that I'm interested in other people's lives, hearing their stories and the events that shaped them. Growing up in a small town in Cornwall it took me a while to accept me, for me. I deliberately chose a college away from school friends as I felt different from them. Then because of that difference I felt, I didn't make connections there. This was true for university, and then I met Tom. We were both introverts and lived in our bubble until that popped. Then the only guys I met were those who I had sex with. I have, or had, it's evolving I guess, intimacy issues with connecting with people. This is changing though, as I move my focus on friendships rather than sexual gratification, I see my confidence gain too. With Adam, I saw myself as boring. I was withdrawn, I couldn't be myself around him. I am a funny person. I am a confident person. I am a good person.

Grindr and other dating apps are not all about hooking up and I've managed to find some good friends during this past year. This is important as I sometimes think who would be at my funeral. When a cousin of mine sadly passed away at a young age his funeral was packed. People gathered outside as there was no room left in the chapel. I picture mine and see just a handful of people. That makes me feel sad as I am capable of making connections, I've proved that to myself and I have a lot to give, but for some reason the choices in my life up to turning forty has not filled me with vast amounts of friends.

I find joy in the simple things like spontaneously meeting a friend for a coffee. I meet with Chris who cannot wait to tell me all about his recent pursuits. He has no filter and no volume control. Everyone in the coffee shop hears and are tuned in to his stories as he loudly tells me, 'and then his girlfriend sends me a message saying leave my boyfriend alone. He's blocked you and he doesn't want any contact from you again. It was like she was treating me as the other man, and I hadn't even done anything.' This related to a guy who he had been chatting to on a Whatsapp group who has come out as being bi but is still in a five-year relationship and Chris had been offering to support him with it.

'It was a cabaret night, and this hot guy was watching me the whole evening. At the end of the night, he came up to me and I shook his hand. I mean, who shakes someone's hand. It was so embarrassing. He gave me his number but the next day I realised it was missing a digit. I'm really gutted as he was so cute too.'

'You'll have to try and track him down on Grindr. Then when you do meet up you'll have a good story to tell the grandchildren.'

'Ha, yes. Guess we will.'

Very simple exchanges but very enriching.

I nearly met Chris as a hook up seven months ago. We had chatted for a while, somewhat flirtatiously, although thankfully I didn't send any nudes, but we arranged to meet for a dog walk. As soon as I met him, we instantly clicked and had so much in common, he's basically an extroverted me. I do think what would have happened if we did meet as a hook up? He would have been part of a long list of one-night stands and that would be just that. Now he's a good friend who I can just chat about nonsense with over a bottle of wine or two. Chris is in the same line of work as me and he ends up applying for a role in my organisation and gets it. We become Work Husbands.

I do dinner parties. I've hardly hosted these before, but it feels good. I love getting comments on how good my cooking is. It turns out I'm a hoot too as we all share dating horror stories as well as other anecdotes of the life of being 40, single and gay. I'm chatty and funny in a way that I couldn't be around Adam. I get invited to other dinner parties and gatherings.

Chris is a bad influence on me. Through Chris I meet Mark. He's the one who did the photos and my now gym buddy. There is a calmness to Mark which I see in myself. I feel very comfortable in his company. We carve out a regular gym session once a week and I quickly learn that Mark is a terrible gossip which I love about him. If we are not gossiping we are eyeing up the muscle lads in the gym. For the first time in ages, or ever maybe, I feel a sense of belonging.

Guess what? I get to go on another holiday. I know, so soon after Mexico. Chris and Mark are desperate to get away, so we opt on a lad's holiday in Gran Canaria. I use the word 'lads' very loosely. Yes, holiday number three. This holiday is filled with absolute giggles, pure relaxation, and a lot of naughtiness. It must be said, I'm quite enjoying this single life.

Chapter 32

Gran Canaria

'It's a cross between Disney Land and Jurassic Park'
– Random One Night Stand, Name Unknown.

Tom and I had visited Gran Canaria about ten years ago but we didn't experience all of what it has to offer, from a gay perspective anyway. Mark and Chris introduced me to the attractions it has. I have to confess, I was quite naive before and didn't realise everything that goes on, this was a holiday of education.

Arriving at our hotel we go straight for a drink. I feel one of the boys which I've never felt before. I was always the camp, shy kid at school and had more girlfriends (platonic obviously) than boyfriends. I didn't come to terms with my sexuality until a lot later. I would fantasise about being asked to stay late and shower with the P.E. teacher but managed to trick my mind that it didn't mean anything. The power of ignorance. I've used that a lot in my life and am now starting to realise I was guilty of that in my relationship with Adam. For shit's sake, how many times must I have written Adam's name? The Word Find function reveals 199. 199 Adams. 200 now. That's a weird image. I realise I'm thinking about him less and less though. He's still there, but a passing thought rather than an all-consuming one.

The days of this holiday are spent lounging in the hot sun whilst the nights are spent partying. This is the club 18-30 holiday I didn't have at eighteen which I'm having at forty. I love it though. After a civilised dinner and Gin and Tonics in the hotel bar we start to get ready for the evening. It's already about ten o'clock and this is the time we are starting to go out. Reverse ten years when I was here with Tom, we would have been having our last cup of tea at this stage before going to bed.

'Are you wearing that?' Chris asks in a slightly judging way.

'What's wrong with it?' I reply in a slightly defensive way. I'm wearing a fitted white t-shirt and white chino type jean trousers. I think I look good.

'It might get a bit dirty.' This is what I had in store for the evening. We go to our separate rooms to get ready and then, when we meet in Chris's room, I'm greeted by them in their sports attire where they look more dressed for the gym than an evening out. Mark's shorts are the shortest I've ever seen on a man with Chris's not far behind. After seeing them, I follow suit and change into my gym clothes which gets an approving nod from Chris.

We arrive at the Yumbo Centre and I feel cheated. It wasn't quite what I was expecting, and the hype Mark and Chris had created in my head. It looked a bit derelict and sad with the seventies flashing sign of a crocodile or dinosaur or newt or sperm or whatever it was meant to be. However, once inside the atmosphere was infectious. Poor choice of last word there.

'We'll do a loop first and get our bearings, then decide where we go for our first drink.'

Every time I hear someone say that phase, 'bearings', I want to make the joke 'you've lost your earrings?' as if I've misheard, but I stop myself as I know it's not funny. As we do our circuit, I feel watched by a zillion bitchy queens. I love it though. It felt more like a catwalk than, well whatever it is. All of the Ls, the Gs, the Bs, the Ts and the Qs and extra letters and symbols which are now included. People dressed in rubber, in leather, in sports, you name it. People old and young all strutting their stuff whilst being watched from the side by those sipping cocktails in the bars that ran the edge of the 'center'. I see a young gay couple holding hands and I think how much easier they have it from when I was eighteen and still coming to terms with my sexuality. Of course, generations before me would probably say the same thing. I hope, and think, future generations won't give this a fleeting thought, that now in western society, being gay is a non-issue for most.

We start with cocktails in a few bars followed by a comedy drag show at Ricky's Bar. Mark is so excited to be back. I fear being picked on at first but soon relax into it and enjoy the show. I don't stick out here, it's the straight woman with the big boobs who gets picked on. 'Excuse me love, are you a lesbian?' asks Drag Queen.

She's clearly not as she holds hands with her husband. 'No' she replies.

'You might want to tell that to your hairdresser then love.'

Delivered with such directness the confidence of the performers is off the scale, and I wonder if the clothes and make up are armour and if they exude the same confidence in everyday life.

We then move to a club. A dancing club that is. By now the cocktails are starting to take effect, especially how they are served in buckets and measures are somewhat looser than in the UK. In fact everything, or everyone is somewhat looser here. I would never dance without alcohol, I know quite sad really, whereas with a few drinks inside me I become John Travolta. I'm probably dancing to my own rhythm but that's fine. Dancing to my own rhythm, I like that. That should become my mission statement. From here we go on to our next club, it's called Cruise and it offers more than just dancing.

As soon as I walk in, I'm nervous and want to pee but I'm worried about going into the toilets on my own. Mark accompanies me and we take it in turns whilst the other stands guard for any unwanted advances. I feel a bit like a schoolgirl at this stage. We decide to all split off for about an hour then to meet up by the bar. There are only two main areas, left or right so I take left, leaving Mark and Chris to work out how they play it. It's very odd walking around and I soon learn there is a rule book to how you work out if you like the other person or not. A look becomes a stare. Turning away becomes exaggerated as if you are looking for something on the floor. A look and slight touch of an arm means, 'yes please.'

It's very dark. A bit too dark for my liking. It

reminds me a bit of the Meadery. Although I'm sure this type of activity does not take place there. As I circuit the establishment my Fitbit awards me a badge for doing so many steps. After a while I decide rather than walk around, I'll stay put and let people find me. I find an empty cubicle and lean against it in a seductive way. In my head anyway, I'm very drunk at this point. It feels incredibly liberating and I feel like a sex worker and that cubicle is my corner. I start to feel possessive about it and anyone who is not my type I see as competition and start giving them evils.

'Move on bitch,' I thankfully only say in my head. After a while a tall, toned older guy in his mid 50s gives me the look and powers over me as I slowly walk backwards in what is now our cubicle.

We intensely stare at each other and start to kiss. He kisses passionately and with force as he starts to caress my body. With just a small light shining down on us the moment intensifies. I can feel my heart pounding as well as my penis getting erect. I lift my t-shirt over my head so I'm still wearing it on the shoulders, which frames my body more. He starts tweaking my nipples as our lips lock in a kiss. He then pushes my head down to sniff his crouch before he unleashes his erect penis for me to suck which I do without hesitation. After a while he lifts me by my arm pits and swings me around so I'm facing the cubicle wall. Here he pulls down my shorts and jock strap before entering me. There is nowhere for me to go but take him as he fucks me from behind. I feel every inch of him enter my body and can't help but scream in pleasure. My head banging against the hard cold surface of the cubicle.

When he is done, I go to dress myself.

'That was really hot,' I tell him.

'I'm Jonathan by the way.'

'I'm Fred.'

Fred, sounds an old name I think to myself but later learn he is from Amsterdam so maybe that's a younger name there? Just as I think we are done he holds me by my penis and directs me out of the cubicle into the bar. I'm holding my shorts and jock so I'm naked but for the t-shirt I am wearing.

'Can I get you a drink?' I'm asked. I still don't really know what is going on.

'A beer,' I reply. This feels odd being so public and naked but there are other guys around in similar attire. As we wait to be served he forces my head back down to his penis as I suck him in full view of everyone. I can't believe I'm doing this but try not to think about it, so I don't stay in my head and instead concentrate on his. Our drinks arrive and as I take a sip of my beer he moves behind me and enters me again. I don't actually think people are watching at this point but nonetheless it feels incredibly racy. He then gets me to sit on his lap as we drink our beers. It is an experience like no other.

Thankfully Chris and Mark missed the show. They were preoccupied with other things. Just after making myself more acceptable by putting clothes on, I say 'more acceptable' as I don't think I quite get to the acceptable level pre-Fred, my dignity is still nowhere to be seen, I see Chris.

'You okay?' I ask.

'No, I've lost my phone. My bank card and everything was with it.'

'When did you have it last?'

'I don't know.'

'Okay where have you been.' I get a blow-by-blow account of where Chris has been, which is an appropriate word to use. Mark joins at this point and we decide to split up and see if we can find it. Pick pocketers are rife in places like this but we decide to search for it in case it did fall from his pocket whilst he was not concentrating.

I use the torch on my phone as a light and it was quite humorous to see these startled guys like rabbits in a headlight. I try and explain I'm looking for a phone but I'm very drunk at this point and can't articulate the right words. I'm tired from all this partying and decide to give up and just get a soft drink at the bar. I know, award for best supportive friend goes to … After a while I feel guilty so decide to look again only to walk in on Chris receiving a blow job in one of the rooms. I giggle to myself. Ten minutes later Chris and Mark

JONATHAN LEE

return and we decide to call it a night. We walk back to the hotel, and I share all the details of my encounter and I count the scares and grazes on my body. 'Your head is bleeding,' Mark points out. It was so worth it though.

***

Poor Chris spent three hours trying to sort his phone and card. It was later used throughout the night, so we suspect it was pinched. He had no recollection of receiving the blow job whilst he was supposed to be looking for his phone and we belly laugh at the events of the night the next morning.

The rest of the evenings were not quite as dramatic or eventful, but we still had a good time. Is this single life though? I contemplate whether this is what I want. To be fair, it's easier than Grindr. I don't have to have the mind-numbing conversations here or the ghosting and catfishing and everything else wrong with social media. Here it's just a glancing stare followed by a yes or no.

Mid-week we decide to go to Café Wein. Chris hears about it from a hook-up. Sitting at the top of what looks like an abandoned shopping centre sits a little café which serves lavish cakes and tea. It was an experience like no other. All the customers were gay men. There was a feeling of belonging which felt good. I'm used to feeling like the outsider, but here I was not.

After cake we return to our spot near the pool where we have a good view of everything that goes on. Mark and Chris love people watching too, although it's kind of adapted to people perving here. I lie on my sun lounger in the blazing heat and 'James – Sit Down' starts on my play list. This was my and Tom's song. I remember just after we split, we went to a concert, and this was played acoustically at the end. It was quite poignant. I think of him for a bit and what we had and then I think of Adam. Adam and I didn't have a song. I'm not sure why. Another song plays, Part: Spiegel Im Spiegal – Fratres – Fur Alina. That's how it's written in my playlist library anyway. I've got eclectic music taste. With the sun warming my body, my body supported by the chair and ground beneath me I lie there for the full eight and a half minutes as I feel at one with myself. Accepting of who I am and what I have.

C h a p t e r 3 3

Phoenix

It's Valentine's Day, the one day of the year where singletons are made to feel even worse about their insignificant existence. The day where couples can stick two fingers up and dwell on co-habiting or boast their loved-up ways and partnerships. I decide I'm not going to spend Valentine's alone; I'm going to go on a date. A date with myself.

I book a Flotation Therapy session. One whole hour of weightlessness submerged in salt water in a pod of complete darkness. I'm seeing this as a date with my innermost thoughts. I'm unsure if I should go naked or wear swimming trunks. I'm too embarrassed to ask so go for the latter. Even with just myself I'm still a prude. As I arrive, I'm greeted by a lovely receptionist who explains how it works. I take a shower; I have fifteen minutes to relax and prepare before heading to the pod where I'll experience mood lighting and relaxing music for the first ten minutes before being completely deprived of my senses where I'll float in darkness. There is a panic button to the left of me, and a lights button to the right should I need it.

I'm too impatient to just sit in a room for fifteen minutes so a quick shower and I submerge myself into the pod and close the lid of the tank. There is something quite cosmic to the whole experience. I float in complete darkness and already I feel relaxed. My mind wonders to what I'm having for tea and then I tell myself off for not having a more profound thought. I've always struggled to meditate. At the end of a yoga class, I can never clear my mind and I'm always planning what I'm doing next. Apart from one time when I did actually fall asleep and embarrassingly had to be woken by the yoga instructor with me lying on my mat in an empty room!

So, what to think about – achievements? Are you where you want to be Jonathan at this point in your life? I don't have an answer for this.

Happiness – are you happy? I think so. Should I buy dungarees? I think they could be a good look for me, but do I have the confidence to pull them off? They would have to be slim cut ones otherwise I'll look like Bob the Builder, or some reject from the Village People.

I like the floating part, but I don't know what to do. I feel myself getting restless. I start to turn around in circles like a fish would do when they are caught in a net. My skin at this point is feeling very silky from the high salt content of the water. I start rubbing my skin and like the sensation. I adjust myself in my swimming trunks and feel myself getting an erection. Would it be wrong if I start masturbating? I know the answer to this, but I do it anyway. It would definitely be wrong to ejaculate, the salt content is already high, but I decide to stroke myself for a bit and feel naughty for doing so. I stop to have deeper, cleaner thoughts.

Sadly, I don't get any profound thoughts or revelations but I do enjoy the experience and I come out feeling relaxed. If nothing else my muscles feel like they've had a good massage and my skin is still shiny and soft to touch. Relaxation over, tick, I have other things to do. It's a day off work and life admin tasks await.

Standing in the queue of the post office seems the most mundane of things. I brought my dad some duty-free fags and am about to get them weighed to send them to him. I brought them for him rather than me as I'm trying to give up. I'm vaping now; just as much satisfaction. Not. Although I do sometimes like to vape on my balcony to give myself the illusion of smoking.

'Can you tell me what's in it?' the post office lady asks. Nosey cow, I think. Why does she need to know. I'm feeling rebellious.

'Yes, they are used underwear.'

The post office lady, who badge reveals the name of Sue looks shocked. 'I'm sorry?'

'Yes, they are used underwear. It's a fetish thing, someone who is into that type of thing is buying them from me.'

There's a pause. There's actually a silence as the Counter 2 stop what they are doing to listen. 'Oh right', and the value?'

'Well, they are actually cheap underwear so the cost to me is only £10 but I'm getting £100 for them.'

'Do you want me to put it down for £10 or £100?'

'Just ten is fine.' I walk out with a smirk on my face. I think I'm trying to get that naughtiness where I can. This is a new thing for me.

There's another change. A bigger change. It took deleting his email and cutting my hair to move on from Adam. The latter happened whilst visiting my mum.

'Just what are you doing with your hair?' My mum so tactfully said. 'It's dry, it's damaged and it looks a mess.'

I reflected for a bit as I looked at myself in the mirror. My hair was scrapped back as it always was. My mum was right. I couldn't argue with her. In truth, I had been keeping it long as that's what Adam said he liked about me. In the back of my head, underneath the mop, I still held onto the thought of us getting back together. That if I was still feeling lost a year on from our split, I'd contact him. I didn't realise at the time, but Fliss later commented that when I cut my hair, she thought I had been holding onto something. She was right and cutting my hair I truly let go of the past.

I blocked his email approximately eleven months after we split. I would periodically get an email from him. They would tend to start nice along the lines of missing me, or thinking of me. However, they always ended toxic. The last one included him saying that he was planning a trip to Greece alone and how he couldn't wait to 'ornate his body which was still fucking hot and bed some seriously good looking guys.' This was the last straw for me. I replied asking him at what point he felt it acceptable to tell me this and that I had worked out how to block emails and after sending this one that is exactly what I planned to do, and I never wanted to hear from him again. In hindsight this is something I should have done months ago. Why was I holding onto dead flowers? That's a metaphor which I can use to describe our relationship. It was beautiful once.

I know I was guilty of trying to hold onto the past. Within the first few months of our separation, I struggled to let go. It was me who messaged him. It was a contradiction as in truth I did not want him back, but I felt that I needed him in my life. I still loved him. Whereas now, I feel indifferent towards him. Yes, I still think about him. He pops into my head occasionally when I'm reminded of him by something such as seeing a teacake or an incense candle. He went a bit hippy towards the end and when he moved into his own flat. I no longer hate him. Overtime these feelings have dissolved. I want him to be happy. I hope he doesn't hate me, although if he does, I don't care. I don't feel responsible for his happiness. There was a time when I did feel this burden.

There is greater awareness through writing. I create understanding. Coupled with time I create distance. I can travel back into those feelings during the first month or two and can see just how much I have moved on. The torture I put myself through, for what? Logically I know that imagining him with other guys achieved nothing good. I just couldn't help myself. I was still in love. It would be interesting to see what feelings would come up if I was to run into him but as I reflect on what we had, and what we were, I feel strong.

Chapter 34

A year to the day

It would have been exactly one year to the day since we split. I want my birthday to be special so plan a fancy meal out with friends. I have friends now. I still feel a pull to Cornwall and my family so visit a week before my birthday so I can spend some time with them too. It's a relatively new thing my family have started to do, but they find it acceptable to do absolutely nothing. Just sitting around, often with alcohol and spend the day in this unstructured way. I want to plan everything otherwise it feels like I haven't achieved anything. If I planned a lazy day in my mum's garden drinking prosecco, then that's fine. I could tick that off the list, but we didn't, so I feel my stresses kicking in.

As a distraction from well the nothingness, I find myself scrolling through Tinder. Same faces as Grindr, except people are more polite on this one. I like the fact that you both must like each other in order to exchange messages, it cuts down on the mind-numbing conversations, although these still exist of course, just with people I find attractive rather than a blank profile box. There are still timewasters, and people trying to sell me bitcoin. I mean seriously do I look that stupid that I'm going in invest thousands to someone whom I've only yet met on a dating site?

Searches are based on location, and I do come across a very handsome guy who, based on his pictures and description, I'm getting sophistication and cultured vibes from. One picture shows him drinking a refreshing sparkling wine against a backdrop of the sea and freshly pressed white table clothes and shiny cutlery. The other shows him driving a fast car. Another of him cuddling his dog in the woodlands. I think I mentioned it earlier, and if I didn't, I was meant to, but one of the things I'm looking for, perhaps slightly superficially, is someone who would look good in a tuxedo. I think

I've found him.

He's called Ewan. I know, sounds a great name. Jonathan and Ewan, I now declare you husband and husband. Oh stop that now. He's 45, good age for me. He works as a manager in retail, I know long hours. He's fluent in seven languages, impressive. He's a dog lover, must be. He's into politics and foreign affairs, okay well I'm sure we will find other things to talk about. He has the same eyes as me. I feel a connection. I instantly swipe right. Nothing happens so he's either not come across me, or he's just not into me. My mind moves to looking at the other inferior guys and like a game I'm swiping left and right as my mum complains about the weather as the sun has gone behind a cloud that looks like an elephant.

About two hours later my phone pings and I see that message I'd been waiting for 'you've got a match.' Thankfully it's not Bob who I accidentally swiped like, a local farmer who by the looks of things has only been growing himself. Although interestingly I never did get a match from him. It was Ewan who immediately follows up with a message. He messages Raff rather than me. Guess my profile must have been very doggy orientated. To be fair I think he was in every photo with me and even one on his own so there were more pictures of him than me. After a few exchanges we start chatting as humans rather than dogs. He's out shopping for home accessories, love that, after recently moving house.

'Why don't you join me for a coffee?' I'm asked. I wanted to go but felt I couldn't abandon my family. I was heading back home the next day so this was our final day of doing nothing together.

'Aww I can't I'm afraid, I'm with my family and we are just about to eat.' A liquid lunch I thought to myself.

'Okay, not to worry, enjoy the family time.' It went quiet for a bit. Is this over before it's even started? About three hours later I send a reply.

'Thinking about it, I'm heading home tomorrow but I'm free for two hours before I visit my aunty if you want to meet for a dog walk.'

I get an instant reply, 'that sounds great, I'd love that.'

Before I have my date, there's another date with my family. An early birthday meal. Not at the Meadery this time, sorry medieval jaunt. I will be back soon though, this time to a restaurant of my choosing. I'm so much more relaxed than last year. I'm able to enjoy it for what it is, my birthday celebration. I feel slightly robbed of my fortieth, I think I'll just erase that year.

The evening is full of giggles and laughter. Oh, and my mum annoying the waiter first to move to the window table that becomes available, then to close the window because it becomes too cold, then to complain about the door being left ajar every time someone leaves or arrives. A few glasses of wine gulped down though, and she soon loosens up and we're fine.

***

Right, it's the next morning so date time now. We arrange to meet at a farm near to a forest which he explains is owned by a friend who is renovating it. 'There is no one there so we can leave the cars and then there are some beautiful walks from there.' I don't question it but in hindsight I've agreed to meet a stranger at a deserted isolated location in the middle of nowhere! You would have thought I'd learn something from watching all twenty-five seasons of Silent Witness.

As I drive to this isolated murder hot spot, I feel slightly nervous which is an unusual feeling for me. I'm not sure if it is anticipation around the date, or concern that he has a shovel in the boot of his car. I finally approach the farm after travelling down what feels like a good mile along a very bumpy road. I see a construction sign telling me to reverse as there is no turning space. I slowly reverse and this takes me forever having to correct my alignment on multiple occasions so a few yards back, a few yards forward and so on. I later find out the construction sign is advising large lorries and not the standard car which I have. Great first impression.

He turns out not to be a serial killer and is the

cultured and well-mannered man which he portrayed himself as on his profile. I talk easily in his company, and we have lots in common. Not in terms of interests, although we do stumble across many common grounds. It's more that our outlooks and the way we think seem to be the same. I think we share similar aspirations, our lifestyles seem to be matched, I feel I can be myself around him. More importantly Raff and his dog, Archie, a collie, get on famously and we spend a beautiful two hours in each other's company as we slowly walk, converse, joke and smile coyly to each other.

At the end of the walk, he asks to kiss me. As he does, he seems less the cultured, defined man but more of a teenager. I see his shyness. We kiss. Afterwards we hug. Then again. I don't want to let him go and I think he feels the same way. Eventually we do depart and as I make my way up the battered, bumpy lane he gets smaller and smaller in my rear-view mirror. I arrive at my Aunty's to a flurry of messages on my phone saying he can't wait to see me again. 'I'm planning on coming back down in two week's time, we could meet up then?'

'That would be amazing,' he replies. I wasn't planning on going back down, but I do, and several times after that.

Chapter 35

My 41st Birthday

It's my birthday! I wake up alone in my bed, but this time I don't feel sad. Last year I wanted the ground to swallow me up. I only felt seventy percent of myself following my split with Adam. In fact, I felt even less than that. I now feel in a happy place, not because of a partner in my life, but because of me.

As I reflect on this past year of my life, I'm struck by the change that has taken place and I want to celebrate this. This book started with my ramblings of my tragic break up with Adam and as my therapy to help me move on. It seems silly to write as I was only with him for two years, but I got so stuck in the cycle of grief. I still cannot fully make sense of this one year on. The hurt, betrayal and anger I felt then has not been matched since, nor has it been felt in those quantities before. This felt very heavy. It's only now as I feel I have walked out of this darkness do I feel lighter.

I'm able to look back at my time with Adam with fondness and think about the good times we shared. I do not regret our time together, and I think about all the learning that I can take from it.

As I started to feel, if not complete again, enough hope to start moving on with my life, I experienced the dating scene and the seedy world of hook ups. We are in the twenty-first century and there is nothing wrong with having fun. I do, however, worry how I have presented the gay world where there are still stigmas around promiscuity. I can, however, only write about my experience, although there is somewhat of a poetic licence to how things happened and it did not quite go Monday to Sunday.

My focus then shifted away from dating as I realised the biggest loss in my life was friendships and meaningful connections. I needed to experience life, and some holidays, and attempting hobbies I learnt how to be myself around others.

My natural default is to withdraw and I'm conscious I need to watch this, as safe and secure as this might feel, it is not fulfilling.

I still miss that feeling of waking up with someone and being close to them. As I've said, I'm not a very tactile person and I need my space at times, okay most of the time. However, I also miss being held. Sometimes I see couples in the street, and I think I want that. They don't even have to be particularly hot couples but if they are then it helps. I will watch them go about their everyday business, sharing a joke, a smile, food, shopping, just anything really. Of course, I know looks are deceiving and when they close the door to the outside world, no one knows what truly goes on and how people feel. You can feel alone in a relationship. I once read (on a Grindr profile but where else do I get my information from), 'it's better to be alone with first class company, then together with second class company.'

I feel I'm now ready for a relationship, but this is not my sole purpose in life. I'm not going to be seventy percent of what someone is looking for. I'm not going to be someone secret. I'm not prepared to compromise. I know there could be a conflict here as realistically all relationships and people will need an element of compromise, although if it feels right, it will feel more like acceptance. If Ewan or another guy is this then great, if not, then so be it.

I want to correct what I said in the opening chapter about people being pretty unremarkable. I don't think that about myself, and I don't think that about others. That was reflective of where I was at the time. I'm grateful that I have moved on from that place, and in doing so I've enjoyed the company of others. You get I'm not talking about sex now, right? I'm talking about how unique we all are, how we are all shaped by our experiences and how we deal with them, and how powerful human connection is.

I hope this book is read and felt by all demographics. Love and loss and how we manage this is not exclusive or defined by a certain gender, sexuality or culture. We all deal with loss in different ways. My way was writing about it. I hope this helps others who are going through similar experiences such as a breakup right now. It is fucking tough though. If I could be so bold to give some advice; be strong, don't wallow in self-pity (or if you do then make it short lived), surround yourself with positive people and do new things. This is your life, and you need to live it. If you are stuck with moving on, find your outlet as to how you can make sense of things. I cannot recommend counselling highly enough, it is a confidential safe space where you can share your inner most feelings. And remember, there is a reason why someone is in your past, don't let that dictate your future like I have been guilty of.

I'm not sure what the future holds. Ewan seems promising as we continue to chat and get to know each other. I realise it was exactly a year to the day when Adam and I split, we matched. I'm not going to romanticise this further. Instead, I'm seeing this as hope. The realisation that I have moved on and can connect. I couldn't have imagined a year ago that I'd be in the place I am now. I feel accepting of myself which puts me in a good place to accept others.

I want to end by sharing my favourite quote. I came across it whilst on a road trip in California with Steve four years ago. We stopped off at a beach for a picnic and were approached by a guy asking for a light who then proceeded to share his life story of once being a Corporate Banker and losing his wealth and now appeared to be living on the beach. I didn't have a light but we continued talking. He shared his Facebook details and told me to befriend him, which I later did. The quote on his front page, which is now on mine, read:

'No cry because cookie is finished. Smile because cookie happened.' – Cookie Monster

Printed in Great Britain
by Amazon

24180439R00159